The Love of Summer

Sarah Thompson

The Love of Summer

Sarah Thompson

Published in Canada by Engen Books, St. John's, NL.

Library and Archives Canada Cataloguing in Publication

Title: The love of Summer / Sarah Thompson.
Names: Thompson, Sarah, 1982- author.
Identifiers: Canadiana (print) 20200165011 | Canadiana (ebook) 2020016502X |
ISBN 9781989473368
   (softcover) | ISBN 9781989473375 (PDF)
Classification: LCC PS8639.H639 L69 2020 | DDC C813/.6—dc23

This book is a work of fiction. Names, characters, places and incidents are
products of the author's imagination or are used fictitiously. Any resemblance
to actual events or locales or persons living or dead is entirely coincidental.

Distributed by:
Engen Books
www.engenbooks.com
submissions@engenbooks.com

First mass market paperback printing: January 2020

Cover Design: Matthew LeDrew

To all the girls I've loved before,
and my wife, the one who I will love forever.

CHAPTER 1

They met at the beginning of the summer of 1999, when Summer moved in next door to Kerri. It was two days after Kerri's 18th birthday. Kerri's blonde hair flowed just over her shoulders, a red ribbon tying it out of her face as she listened to her new TLC CD, burned compliments of Napster, while photographing the newly bloomed tulips in the flowerbed beside her house. Lightly tanned from late afternoons in the sun, she blushed when their eyes first met. Summer immediately noticed the freckles that pebbled over Kerri's nose.

Kerri could feel the blood rushing to her ears, turning them the same colour as her sweater. Summer smiled, slightly averting her eyes, as she made her way up the stoop of her new home for the first time. She would be celebrating her 19th birthday in this new house. After her father hurt his back, her parents had been forced to sell their farm. Summer had taken a year off to help before going to college, but it still wasn't enough, and they had to sell to pay their debts.

Summer had already enrolled in Jenkinstown College when her mother, Joan, had informed her that she had a job offer in the same town. So, Summer decided she would continue living at home to save money while she attended school. It would give her more of a chance to focus on her studies if she didn't have to get a job to pay for an apartment.

Summer ran her thumbs over her ears and her hands over the top of her head, pushing back her long dark hair. It hung halfway down her back and straight as a whip. She dressed in tight-fitting jeans and a knitted sweater. She was unlike anyone Kerri had ever laid eyes on before.

Kerri felt a surge of adrenaline as she continued to stare at the new neighbour. Her heart rate surged, and she barely contained a squeak of excitement as she ran up the stairs and into the house, slamming the door behind her.

The moving van pulled up to the curb in front of the red two-storey home. The house was much the same as all the others in the neighbourhood, each had their own unique colour, but they were all laid out the same. From the porch Summer could see into the window that was to be her parent's bedroom on the left, and through the picture window which led into the formal parlor on the right. Her parents had already started to unpack the boxes the moving men were bringing in.

In front of the house, a small white picket fence separated their driveway from the neighbour's, a constant as Summer looked up and down the street. There were ten houses on the block in total, each with the same construction style and same fence out front. She guessed they had all been built at the same time when the neighbourhood was developed.

Summer entered through the already open front door pausing for only a minute at the large picture window before ascending the stairs to what was to become her new room. She could hear the echo of her foot falls in the empty house and her eyes started to well up with tears as she glanced around at the bare, peach coloured walls. She moved toward the window and glanced at the view, almost directly into the bedroom of the girl who lived next door.

Kerri looked out her window and caught a quick glimpse of the new girl as she began to make her first impression of her new home. Kerri could see the sadness in her eyes and felt a lump of panic forming in her throat. Her heart was still beating as quickly as if she had run a marathon and her breath caught as their eyes met for a brief moment.

Summer turned quickly from the window when she saw the girl next door looking back at her. She made her way down over the stairs and out into the back garden instead. A tire swing hung from the large oak tree in the far corner of the yard. The remainder of the garden was knee high grass. She paused before heading for the swing.

Kerri continued to stand at the window, looking into the empty room and hoping to catch another glimpse of her new neighbour when she saw her out of the corner of her eye, running into the back yard. She felt an unfamiliar nervousness as she worked to slow her breathing, checking her appearance in the mirror before heading back down over the stairs and outside to her own back yard.

Kerri watched the girl through a gap in the fence, waiting for a good time to strike up a conversation. There were no other girls her age in the area. She had grown up with her brother and his friends on their street. Although she loved playing street hockey and baseball with the boys, she had always struggled to make friends with the girls in her class at school. She had longed for another girl her age to talk to.

Summer was lost in thought, letting the tire swing

take her in aimless circles, pushing off the ground occasionally to help it continue the motion. She looked toward the neighbouring yard and noticed another girl's eyes through the fence.

"Who's there?" She moved from the swing and took a couple of hesitant steps towards the fence.

"Kerri Walters. Are you okay?" Her slight voice was barely audible over the distance between them. She squeezed through the hole and stood facing Summer.

"I'm Summer Donnelly." She wiped the tears from her eyes. "Yeah, I'm alright. It just hasn't been the greatest day for me, that's all."

Although Kerri was close to six foot, Summer towered over her. They were as different as day and night, one blonde, the other with hair so black it was almost blue. The girls stood quietly for a moment. Kerri scuffed her foot in the long grass and Summer watched her make the motion, cringing a little when the toe of her Doc Martin would rub the dirt.

Summer reached out and touched Kerri on the forearm. "You're going to ruin the look of your boots if you keep that up," Kerri looked up at Summer and smiled, suddenly realizing what she had been doing. "I mean, they're your boots, but they won't look half as cool all scuffed up."

Kerri felt her face flush again as she focused on the hand that remained on her arm. Summer quickly pulled back when she realized Kerri was staring and giggled a little. It didn't take long before they fell into casual conversation as though they had known each other their whole lives. Kerri felt a connection between them like nothing she had felt with anyone else and they became inseparable.

The long summer nights were spent lying in the grass in deep conversation or taking a trip to the national park to go camping on the weekends. Kerri felt from their first encounter that this relationship was different from any of the other friends in her life. She couldn't spend enough time with Summer to feel satisfied, and every time they touched or hugged she felt a shiver in her knees and a dampness in the palms of her hands.

Kerri could only find one word to describe how she was feeling: Confused. She had never felt like this before and she didn't know what it meant or what she was supposed to do about it. She was only sure that the one thing that she couldn't do was talk to Summer about it, even though they told each other everything. Kerri had even told Summer about the time her brother, Jack, had tried to kill his best friend, Davey, for asking her out.

"I didn't really care that he asked, I just wasn't interested in going out with him. He is nothing but a big oaf. Besides, I don't know why he would ever be interested in me, you know?"

"I'm sure there are lots of guys that are interested in you, you just don't notice." Summer replied, placing her hands behind her head as she lay back in the grass to look at the sky.

"Not really. Just Davey, and even though Jack warned him to stay away from me, he just kept following me around like a lost puppy all year. I mean, I get why Jack was angry about it, Davey is a couple of years older than me, and he is Jack's best friend, so even if he wasn't older it would probably be weird for Jack if we started dating." Kerri sat with her legs folded under her as she pulled blades of grass from the ground.

"That makes sense. I guess it doesn't really matter if

you aren't interested anyway. So, ah, classes start tomorrow. Are you nervous?"

"Nah. It's going to be great."

***

The first day at Jenkinstown College was a hard one for Summer. This was the first time the pair had been apart since she moved to town. She knew they would share some courses, but most of their time would be spent in different buildings on the campus as they were taking different programs. When she arrived in front of the English building with Kerri on the first day, Summer could feel a knot burning in her stomach and a wave of nausea floating up inside her when they parted.

At the end of the day the girls met in front of the same building. Kerri threw her arm around Summer's shoulder when she got close enough. "How was the first day?" Kerri smiled slyly at her, not really expecting an answer.

Summer just smiled back, "Forget today, let's just go home." she grasped Kerri's hand, pulling her a little closer in the process.

Davey ran up behind them, "Well hello ladies, beautiful afternoon. Ah, Kerri, I was wondering if I could talk to you... alone." The Jenkinstown College Student Union Back to School Bash was the following week and Davey clearly had his heart set on taking Kerri.

"I don't know, that depends. What is so important you can't tell me in front of Summer?" She pulled her arm from around Summer's shoulders and stuffed her hands in her pockets. "Anything you want to talk to me about you can do now... or not at all."

Davey's ears started to turn pink as he looked from one girl to the other. "Um, well, see, the thing is, I was wondering if, you know, if maybe..." He still trailed behind them slightly and had trouble to keep up the pace Kerri was setting for them.

"Are you going to spit it out? We're almost home, and we," she gestured to herself and Summer, "have things to do and talk about."

Davey picked up his pace to a near jog and made his way in front of them, taking Kerri by the arm to stop her from proceeding any further. "Go to the Bash with me."

Summer looked at Kerri in surprise, she was under the impression he had given up on her once she started ignoring him entirely over the summer. "Dave, we've been over this. I'm not interested in you, and I certainly wouldn't be caught dead at the Bash with you. Besides, what would Jack do if he even knew you were asking me this?"

"C'mon Ker, it's different now, last year you were only 17 when I asked, and I understand why he was upset. Is it someone else? Do you already have a date, 'cause you can tell me if that's the problem."

"And what if I told you there was someone else?" Without meaning to, she felt her eyes move toward Summer. "Not that I'm saying there is someone else. Just," For once, Kerri found herself stumbling over her words.

"Then if there isn't someone else, why won't you go with me?"

Summer was shifting awkwardly beside them as she waited to hear what Kerri would say, Kerri could see she was getting uncomfortable as she struggled for the words to tell him to mind his own business and leave her alone.

"Because you're nothing but a big oaf who follows my brother around like he is a God and I would rather have someone who is their own person." She grabbed Summer by the hand, "C'mon, let's go to my place."

The two girls headed off towards the house, leaving Davey standing on the sidewalk, hanging his head. Summer couldn't help but feel sorry for the guy. She couldn't understand why Kerri had been so blunt about it. There were better ways to tell him to back off. Besides, he was cute, there was really no reason for Kerri not to go to the dance with him.

They entered the Walters home and headed directly up over the stairs and into Kerri's room. Summer dropped her book bag and flopped down on the edge of the bed. "You didn't have to be so mean to him. I think you really hurt his feelings."

"Davey? Nah, he's tough. Besides, there are lots of girls that would love to go out with him." Kerri sat down beside Summer.

"He looked rather upset to me. And, as near as I can tell, it's only you he's interested in." Summer felt strange talking to Kerri about a guy. Although they had been so close over the last three months, the subject had never come up before and now that it had, Summer realized she didn't want to talk about it. "Anyway, who cares. It's not like I would have anyone to go with. If you're not going, maybe we could watch videos and make popcorn instead?"

"Sounds great to me." Kerri felt her face flush. The now somewhat familiar, but still strange, excitement started to build in her. She had to force herself to keep her breathing steady. Kerri pulled out her books and belly flopped onto the bed, flicking through the required reading for the year.

***

The Saturday of the Bash, Kerri made an extra effort to make everything perfect for when Summer arrived.

She wondered if it seemed strange to be going through so much trouble just to watch a movie with her best friend. Kerri was filled with so much nervous excitement that she almost jogged as she headed to Jenkinstown Convenience at the end of the block to make the video selection.

Nothing seemed like the right thing to watch. American Pie was the newest comedy, but it seemed too corny. Summer hated scary movies, so The Sixth Sense and The Mummy were out of the question. Kerri didn't really want to get a romantic movie, but she stood for a while holding a copy of 10 Things I Hate About You and She's All That, contemplating. The idea of sitting through a Rom-Com with Summer brought a lump to her throat and made her start to question what was really happening with their relationship.

Kerri wanted nothing more than to talk to Summer about how she was feeling, but she was so afraid of how she would react. Jenkinstown was small and the only place she had ever seen a gay person was on television. Realizing that she was having these kinds of feelings made her worry about the gossip around town if anyone found out, or the way her other friends would react if they knew. Thinking about what it would mean made it seem like everything was crashing down around her.

It was like she didn't know how to talk to Summer with these feelings still stirring around inside. As long as she didn't think about it, their conversations were so easy, but the second they were quiet for too long, she couldn't keep herself from wondering what exactly the feeling was.

Finally, she settled on The Matrix after finding the last copy hiding behind Eyes Wide Shut. She hoped action adventure would keep their attention and she wouldn't have to do too much talking. With the video decided on, she stared at the snack rack in the store. She picked up two bags of Cool Ranch Doritos, and chocolate covered raisins, Summer's favorites. It was going to be perfect.

Kerri could barely eat, even though her mother had made her favourite meal, sweet and sour chicken. No one seemed to notice that she was mostly pushing the food around her plate, or that, for once, she wasn't asking for a second helping before anyone else had even finished their first. She quickly cleared the plates at the end of the meal, hoping no one would notice how hard she was working to burn off her nervous energy.

Instead of helping with the dishes, Jack was getting ready to head out to the Bash with his new girlfriend, Martha. Kerri could tell he was trying to make a good impression solely based on the amount of cologne he was wearing. The phone rang and a few minutes later her father was calling them downstairs.

"So, that was Mom's work friend, Joanne, on the phone. She is having a little impromptu gathering this evening and we are going to head out for a couple of hours." Jim grinned. It had been weeks since they had done anything on the weekend besides sit around the house and watch television. "We should be heading out within the hour."

Kerri was suddenly stomach sick. She and Summer would have the house to themselves. She couldn't help but wish that she had actually eaten her supper so there would be something to throw up. Even after spending almost every day and night together since the beginning of the summer, Kerri was getting more nervous every time they were truly alone.

Summer arrived just as Kerri's parents were putting on their shoes and Kerri felt flustered as she quickly explained their plan for the evening.

"Hi Eileen, hi Jim! Have a good time." Summer exclaimed with a wave as they moved toward the door.

"We will. Now, you girls don't stay up too late and make sure the door is locked before you go upstairs." Jim was always concerned about the door being locked, even though it was a safe neighbourhood.

"Dad, we aren't little kids anymore. You don't need to worry so much," Kerri said. She was worried, but not about what time it would be when they called it a night. She was worried about whether or not she should talk to Summer about what she was feeling. Summer was still taking off her boots when Kerri disappeared from the room.

Summer found Kerri in the rec room, already on the couch, working the DVD remote to set up the movie. They usually watched movies in Kerri's room, but the Walters' recently purchased a DVD player and they weren't allowed to move it upstairs. Summer planted herself down on the cushion beside Kerri and started picking at the raisins on the coffee table.

"Is somebody dying? You have all my favorites. Last time I came home to something like this it was because we were moving," she laughed a little and looked up at Kerri.

Kerri smiled at her, "No, nothing like that, I just figured, if you are going to miss your first college bash to watch videos with me, I had better make it worth your while." She started to blush and hoped Summer wouldn't infer anything from the comment. Or maybe she hoped that she would.

"Let's just watch the movie." Summer patted the couch beside her for Kerri to move closer.

Kerri had been slowly shifting toward the arm of the couch and further away from Summer, not wanting to get too close. She also didn't want to deal with the heavy feeling in her chest when their thighs touched. Each day Kerri spent with Summer made her happier than she had ever been. She never wanted to feel the way she did - Summer was her best friend. She was afraid of ruining everything because, more than anything in the world, she treasured their connection and finally having a female friend to talk to.

Kerri hit play and decided that she couldn't say anything. Not that night, not ever. She still had no idea what her feelings meant, only that she couldn't let them get in the way of the relationship that they were building. She had been pushing the feelings down for a while and she convinced herself that she could continue to do so.

CHAPTER 2

Kerri worked hard every day to keep her feelings to herself, not just in her words, but in her actions toward Summer. She had been able to keep the stopper on the bottle, but it was starting to take a mental toll. There were a few occasions where she had become angry and lashed out at anyone and everyone around her. It seemed like it was coming out of nowhere most of the time. Her family and friends couldn't understand her reasons because she was too afraid to say it out loud.

Kerri had even found herself snapping at Summer a couple of times. The hurt expression on her face made Kerri quickly apologize, and despite Summer's pleading, she always insisted there was nothing wrong.

One of her outbursts led to her screaming at her mother, something she had never done.

"Kerri, I think you need to start spending more time out of the house. With the exception of school, and the time you spend with your camera, you barely go out at all anymore. I know you hang out with Summer, but you have so many more friends. And, I can't remember the last time you went out on a date." Eileen was getting frustrated and wanted to help Kerri be in a better mood.

"Do you ever think that I just don't have anyone that

I'm interested in dating? Or that I would rather spend my time alone that with a bunch of fake people. Besides, If I'm going to be a famous photojournalist someday, I need all the practice I can get."

"But honey, that doesn't mean you should stop living your life. I know Jack thinks it's weird, but Davey is a nice boy and he seems to like you a lot."

"How many times do I have to tell you that I'm not interested in dating any boys right now? Why can't you just leave me the hell alone for a change and worry about living your own life!" Kerri ran up the stairs to her room and slammed the door, her mother right at her heels.

Eileen threw the door open and marched over to where Kerri was lying face down on the bed. "Now, young lady, there is absolutely no need for screaming at me and your father. You were more mature than this when you were a pre-teen. I don't know what crawled up in your hole, but you better get it out in a hurry if you plan to continue to live under this roof."

Kerri just looked at her, "I'm sorry," she whispered. "I don't know why I reacted like that. Something just came over me."

"Well whatever it is, you need to figure it out. I will not be disrespected in my home, not even by my child." Eileen's eyes softened as Kerri turned to look at her again. "Kerri, is something bothering you?"

"I'm fine. I'm just really sorry. Would you mind letting me be alone for a while?"

"Okay. But you still need to apologize to your dad." Eileen walked out of the room and clicked the door closed behind her.

As much as she regretted it after the fact, as much as she knew she was acting like a child, Kerri couldn't make it stop or predict when an outburst would happen. The one thing she felt sure of was the only thing that would end the frustration was for her to be honest about her feelings and let her secret out.

Kerri wanted nothing more than to forget about how she was feeling, but she couldn't help but dwell on it when she was alone. The more Kerri explored what these feelings meant to her, the more she realized she had felt something like this before. It gave her a different perspective on a lot of things that had happened in her life. It gave her a new outlook on almost everything around her.

As Kerri looked around her room, she thought about why she had chosen the posters for her walls and realized the reasons probably weren't very different from those of other teens. Some because she admired them and some because she was attracted to them. She looked over at a Melissa Etheridge poster, pictures of Neve Campbell and Shannon Doherty torn from old Teen Beat and Tiger Beat magazines and a full-size Buffy the Vampire Slayer poster on another wall. Sure, she had a picture of Kurt Cobain and Courtney Love, but Kurt was half covered by a list of inspirational quotes that she had printed in the library at school.

She could remember being embarrassed to give a valentine to the most popular girls in elementary school, even though they had to give one to every student in their class. She even had a new realization about why she was so excited about the leather jacket that Kelly McGillis was wearing in the movie Top Gun, or the one that Michelle Pfeiffer had donned in Dangerous Minds. It even suddenly made sense why she was so excited the first 20 times she had watched Wild Things.

It was nearing the Christmas break and the Jenkinstown College Student Union had many activities and events planned to end the semester, including a formal Gala for students and faculty to mingle. Kerri had been avoiding Davey as much as possible since the announcement. She really didn't want to have to deal with him asking her out, once again, especially now that she was starting to figure things out about herself.

A week before the formal Summer met Kerri outside the English building, as they did every day, but this time there was something different about Summer. Her ears were a little pink and a look of shock was spread across her face.

"Kerri, you won't believe it." Summer couldn't quite look her in the eyes, choosing instead to focus on her feet and scrape the bottom of her Airwalks along the edge of the sidewalk. "Phil just asked me to the Gala."

Kerri couldn't breathe and for a minute she thought she would throw up, right then and there. She knew the day would come when this would happen, when some guy would come along and come between them. The day that she either had to accept that friendship was all they had, or slowly let Summer slip out of her life. Summer was too caught up in having a date for the formal to pay much attention.

Kerri was quiet all the way home that day. Summer more than made up for her silence, running on about what dress to wear and if he would bring a corsage. She hardly noticed the pain on Kerri's face or her silence.

The following day Davey cornered her on the way to meet Summer outside the English building. "I know I'm probably wasting my breath, but I'm going to try this one more time."

Kerri stopped in her tracks, looking up at him. "Fine,

go ahead."

"Kerri, the Gala is coming up on the weekend, and I was wondering if you would like to accompany me?"

Kerri felt her heart break a little as she thought about Summer going with Phil. There was nothing that made her want to go out with Davey, but if Summer had a date, she felt that she needed one as well. "Fine," she replied grudgingly.

It was in the moment she said yes that she realized the only person she wanted to be with was the girl next door, but that was never going to happen. Kerri repeated it over and over in her head, trying to convince herself that she couldn't tell Summer or anyone else what she was going through. She tried to convince herself that the only way she was going to feel better was if she cut Summer out of her life altogether. If Kerri couldn't be the one Summer wanted to be with, then she couldn't be her friend either. She headed home that day without waiting for Summer. She went straight to her room and started to cry thinking about having to keep pretending to be something she was not and continuing her charade on top of losing her friend.

There was a knock at her bedroom door and a soft voice echoed from behind it. "Kerri, can I come in?"

Kerri recognized Summer's voice and wanted nothing more than to be able to talk to her about what was causing her so much pain. She shook her head at the idea, collected herself and wiped her eyes before responding. "Come in."

Summer entered slowly and sat down beside her on the bed. "You didn't wait for me after class, is everything alright?"

"I'm just not feeling the greatest, that's all. Have you

picked out your dress for the Gala?" Kerri choked out the words, rolling onto her back to look at the ceiling as she waited for the response.

"Yeah, I think so, its black and knee length, but mom still wants me to wear the pink one. Did I hear you finally agreed to go out with Davey?"

Kerri fought hard to hold back the sobs. "Yeah... I'll give him one thing, he's persistent." She choked on the last word and pulled the pillow into her chest, breathing deep.

"Ker, what is it?" A look of concern crossed Summer's face. She lightly brushed the bang from Kerri's eyes, running her fingers softly down the side of her cheek as she did. "If you don't want to go out with him, why did you agree to it?"

Kerri looked up at her. She wanted to melt into her eyes, but all she could do was try to smile. "I might as well go, what else am I going to do?" Kerri could feel the anger start to grow inside her once again. "What do you care anyway? Why don't you just go home and call your boyfriend."

She rolled to face the wall. Summer's face dropped. Touching her lightly on the shoulder, she rose from the bed and left the room. Kerri broke into tears when the bedroom door closed, and she realized Summer had really left. She was pushing her away because she honestly believed the only way she was going to be able to move forward would be to leave Summer behind.

Kerri wanted so badly to pick up the phone and call her, apologize for how she had acted and ask her to come back. Instead she just looked out the window, waiting to see Summer enter her bedroom. She watched for a couple of hours before her mother called her for supper. There was no sign of the girl who, without even knowing it, had destroyed her heart in an instant.

For the rest of the week, Kerri avoided all contact with Summer. She wanted nothing more than for things to be the way they had been just a week before. She couldn't sleep, thinking about her feelings for Summer and wondering why she had to go through this. Kerri fought an unending internal battle between keeping her feelings a secret forever and needing to tell Summer how she felt. Her greatest fear remained knowing that telling Summer anything would create even more tension between them than she already had.

That weekend, Kerri grudgingly got dressed for the dance. The only thing that made her smile about the idea was the chance to see Summer in her dress, and maybe an opportunity to tell her how stupid she had been. It might be a chance to apologize for how she had behaved the last time they saw each other and how she had acted since.

Despite trying to convince herself that she wanted to keep Summer out of her life entirely, there was something in Kerri that couldn't let her go, that wouldn't allow her to shake Summer from her thoughts. Without realizing it, Kerri had built her life around Summer, everything from wearing the shirts that she liked, to planning her classes so they would be finished at the same time each day.

Kerri held back tears as she took another look at herself in the mirror. Davey wasn't a bad guy, she could do much worse, and if she was going to have to live her life in a lie, without being honest about who she loved, at least there was someone who loved her.

He would be there to pick her up any minute and Kerri was still trying to straighten out her tights. The last time she had worn a pair was when her grandmother died the year before. Her mind wandered to the feeling of cold that hung over the church and the grayness of her grandmother's skin while she struggled to get the toe to line up correctly. She had always despised dressing up and sputtered to herself under her breath about why she had ever agreed to go to the Gala in the first place.

Her mother's voice filtered up over the stairs, "Kerri, your date is here. Shall I have him take a seat, or are you almost ready?"

Kerri gave herself one more look to make sure that every hair was in place and brushed her bang out of her eyes. No matter how much she hated getting into these outfits, she knew that she could make it look good and she pushed back the thought that she wanted Summer to see that too. "I'm coming, I'm coming," She shouted back to her mom.

Kerri gave Davey her best fake smile and crossed her arms over her chest as they walked the few blocks to the school to prevent him from reaching for her hand. They walked into the Gala and Kerri immediately started scanning the crowd for any sign of Summer. She caught a glimpse of Summer's dress as she made her way across the dance floor to the Ladies room. Kerri gave Davey a quick excuse and followed after her.

Kerri rushed through the swinging door and found herself in a bathroom crowded with girls touching up their makeup or hair as they arrived. It was a tight squeeze and she felt the uncomfortable feeling she always had when entering a public washroom as she pushed through the crowd to locate Summer.

Two and three at a time, the girls started to filter out of the bathroom and back to their dates. Kerri wiped the counter with a paper towel and sat herself on the sink.

Summer had not been with any of the groups as they left, so Kerri decided to wait until she emerged from one of the stalls. Soon, she was the only one in the room and when the swinging door closed, Kerri could hear sobbing from the furthest stall down.

"Summer?"

The girl sniffed and breathed hard but did not reply.

"Are you in there? It's Kerri. Come out, I want to talk to you."

Kerri could hear the pain in her voice as she responded. "What do you want?"

She leaned against the stall and lowered her voice. "I told you, I just want to talk to you. Listen, I'm really sorry about how I've been acting all week. I shouldn't have shut you out just because you agreed to go to the dance with Phil."

"Is that what this is all about? Why do you care if I go out with him? It's not like you want to." The door swung open and Kerri fell forward into Summer. For a moment she forgot about everything and everyone else and stared into Summer's eyes. In that moment the world seemed to revolve only around the girl in front of her.

Kerri steadied herself on her feet and tried to collect her thoughts as Summer watched, coming to her own conclusion. "Is that the problem? Are you interested in Phil?"

Kerri was speechless, something only Summer could seem to do to her. She took a deep breath and tried to figure out the right words, any words that weren't her true feelings. "No, of course I'm not interested in Phil. Don't you think I would have said something before now if I had feelings for him?"

"Jesus Ker, will you just tell me what the hell it is that

is making you so mad at me? I didn't do anything to hurt you as far as I can tell, and there is certainly no need for you to be jealous of some guy I agreed to go to this stupid Gala with." Summer brought her hand to rest lightly on Kerri's shoulder. "Why can't you just talk to me?"

Kerri could feel the warmth of the tears that dripped from her eyes and, although she knew that she should, she didn't try to prevent them. The words came hard and fast through the sobs, almost in a shout. "I don't know how to tell you what it is. You wouldn't understand." Kerri pressed her back against the cool tile of the wall and lowered her body, using the wall to guide her to the floor.

Summer looked confused and concerned as she quickly sat down in front of Kerri, unsure as to whether she should reach for her hand or keep her distance. "Why not? Tell me, what could it possibly be that I wouldn't understand?"

"I'm not interested in Phil… or Davey for that matter." Kerri couldn't bring herself to look into Summer's eyes, eyes that she had already memorized. Instead she studied the floor tiles as though she would be tested on their number and design.

"Kerri, I'm here for you no matter what. I don't know what I would have done when I moved here if I hadn't met you." Summer leaned forward to be closer to her friend, pulling her into a tight grasp.

"Sum, I don't know how to explain other than to say everything that has been going on with me is all about you." She swallowed hard at the statement, not sure she had been clear, but knowing it was the most she could manage to say at this point.

"I don't know why or how it would be about me, Ker. I'm here for you and I always will be, no matter what."

She let go of her grip and pulled back slightly to observe Kerri's expression. Summer hoped that by searching in her eyes, she would be able to get a glimpse into what was going on in Kerri's head.

"But it is about you. I thought I had it all figured out until you showed up in my life and now look at me," the sobs started to grow. "Summer, I don't know what to say to make you understand."

Summer looked at her in bewilderment, her heart rate increasing as she guessed at what Kerri had meant by her statement. She focused on the same square on the floor where Kerri was staring and took a deep breath before lifting Kerri's chin so she could look her in the eyes to reply. "Are you saying you don't want me to go out with Phil because you want there to be something between me and you?"

For the second time in a week, Kerri couldn't breathe. She pulled herself quickly from the floor and ran out of the bathroom. Just outside the door she turned back to see if Summer was following her and ran directly into Davey.

"Hey girl! I thought you were after leaving me here." He grinned, oblivious to the tear streaks on Kerri's face. "How about a dance?"

Kerri looked back again as Summer came out of the washroom. She grabbed Davey by the wrist and led him out onto the dance floor. Summer watched as Kerri pushed through the crowd and suddenly realized all she wanted to do was go home. Summer made her way back toward the table where she had left Phil when they arrived.

She walked up to find Phil with a couple of guys in his program, downing a bottle of vodka. "I guess I see how this night is going to go. You promised you weren't going to drink. You said you would drive me home." Summer grabbed her purse and marched out the door of the Student Union.

"Summer, wait." Phil called after her but when she didn't turn, he simply shrugged and sat back in his chair.

Summer planted herself on the cold concrete steps, trying to gather her thoughts. She wanted to go home, but she didn't want to have to answer too many questions from her parents about why she was home so soon, or how things had gone with Phil. Summer kept repeating her conversation with Kerri over and over in her head. Kerri hadn't answered her with words but walking away in that fashion said everything to Summer that she needed Kerri to say. She hadn't realized it, but it was everything she wanted Kerri to say.

Summer felt a warming, like hot chocolate in your stomach on a cold day, when she thought how it would feel to be with Kerri. Even still, she couldn't shake the idea that something about the way she was feeling was wrong. She shook her head, thoughts and emotions falling over her a mile a minute. She couldn't be that kind of girl. It was too complicated for them to be together.

When she turned to see Kerri heading out the door of the Student Union, she changed her mind. Summer took one look at her and knew everything could be alright as long as they faced it together. "Kerri, wait..." Summer shouted after her as Kerri barreled down over the stairs and started along the sidewalk. Summer struggled to catch up.

Davey came running up behind the two, his tie undone, and his jacket thrown over his shoulder. Kerri heard them both behind her and stopped quickly, turning to face them. "Davey, you first. You are an ass. I mean that. A complete ass. Maybe you could keep a girl if you could learn to keep your hands to yourself." Her face flushed in anger. Summer just looked over at him, confused.

"As for you..." Kerri's resolve softened and her anger started to lift as she looked at Summer, "C'mon. Let's go home." Kerri turned around and started for home with Summer right on her heels, leaving Davey still standing in place.

"Kerri, why did you run out of the bathroom?" Summer's high heels made it a struggle for her to keep up with the frantic pace Kerri was setting. "You didn't answer my question. Well, I guess you already had, but you didn't even give me a chance to take anything in, never mind respond to you."

"Just forget it, alright? I shouldn't have said anything. I'm just being stupid, and I didn't want to share my best friend with some stupid guy who thinks the most fun you can have is to go to the formal and drink until you throw up all night."

Summer shuddered. Maybe she had misunderstood their conversation. "But I thought... I mean, didn't you say..."

Kerri could feel the fear creeping over her and decided to try to pretend that nothing had happened. Try to pretend that nothing had been said. "I don't know what you thought I meant, but I'll be glad if you tell me you aren't going to see him again."

Summer nodded in agreement. "Of course not. What a jerk. What happened with Davey in there?"

Kerri chuckled, "He was drinking with the boys while I was in the washroom. I guess it made him a little too confident. He had the gall to grab my ass while we were dancing."

Summer started to laugh at the idea. "I'm surprised

you didn't belt him right then and there." She put her arm around Kerri.

Kerri tried to sound tough and pushed out her chest a little as she spoke. "Well, you know, I would have... but mom would have killed me if I got blood on this dress, it's the only one I own." She couldn't help but smile as Summer pulled her closer into the embrace.

Kerri focused on the way Summer's arm felt around her as they walked the short distance from the College to home. They were a few feet from Summer's front door when she dropped her hold on Kerri, feeling suddenly conscious that people could see them touching.

"Well, we don't have to go in, you know. No one is expecting us this early. Maybe we could keep walking and you could tell me what you were really trying to say in the bathroom?" Summer almost pleaded. She was suddenly both confused and hopeful about what could happen and wanted to figure out what was actually going on between them. "I'm heading to my grandparents for the holidays in the morning and I would really like to talk about it before I leave."

"There really is nothing to talk about." Kerri took Summer by the hands, but quickly dropped them again. "I was just being stupid, and you misunderstood. It's fine. I'll see you when you get back." She dismissed her.

Kerri could see Summer's shoulders drop as she turned and headed toward her front door. "Sure, see you after the New Year."

CHAPTER 3

Kerri's days were long and her nights were sleep deprived and restless over the holidays. She had joined her family at every opportunity when they went visiting cousins or neighbours. She had even spent several afternoons at the Jenkinstown Mall with her mother to pass the time, making the days a little shorter. She was feeling the loneliness of Summer being away and couldn't stop thinking about how unsettled they had left things that night after the Gala.

There were even a couple of nights that she spent sitting at her desk, looking through the window into Summer's room and wishing that she could talk to her, even for a couple of minutes. She would practice the whole conversation in her head, finding a way to tell Summer all the reasons why she lied about her feelings. The time and distance between them made it clear to Kerri in the middle of the night that she needed to be honest, but that clarity changed every morning in the light of day.

She still longed to know that their friendship was okay after she had practically stormed away, but she also struggled with the fact that she wished she could take back that night entirely. She wanted to erase the whole week that she had spent avoiding Summer before the Gala, so that maybe, just maybe, the conversation never would have happened in the first place.

She moped about the house most of the first week that Summer was away and barely ate. Her mom knocked on her door but didn't wait for a reply before letting herself in. "Kerri, honey, I really wish you would talk to me about whatever it is that is bothering you."

Kerri choked back her tears. "Nothing's wrong Mom, I swear. I'm just not feeling the best." It wasn't really a lie. Her stomach had been in knots for days and her head ached from crying when she wasn't able to sleep at night.

"I don't believe you," Eileen sat herself on the end of the bed. "Did something happen at the Gala? Is it about Davey?"

Kerri huffed, "No, Mom it doesn't have anything to do with Davey. I told you, I'm fine."

"Okay. All I can do is ask. If you do want to talk about it, I'm here anytime. You really can tell me anything. I don't know if I'll be able to help, but I will certainly listen."

"I know. I just have a lot on my mind. I'm really alright." Kerri looked her in the eyes, trying to convince her mother.

Her mom rose from the bed. "Summer will be back next week. Maybe you will talk to her if you don't want to talk to me."

Kerri looked quickly out the window, squeezing her fingernails into her hand to keep her composure. "Yeah, maybe." She looked back just as her mom closed the door.

Kerri kept to herself more and more after the conversation with her mom, raging at anyone who even bothered to knock on her bedroom door to see if she was okay.

Things didn't get any better when Davey turned up at the house with a present for her and a black eye.

"Hey, I just wanted to see how you were doing and bring you this," Davey thrust a gift bag in her direction. "It's a combo Merry Christmas and I'm sorry?"

"Nice shiner, what happened?" Kerri replied.

"Jack didn't tell you? I guess you let him in on why you were so mad at me at the Gala and he decided if we were still gonna be friends, this is what I deserved." Davey chuckled. "I s'pose he was right. I did deserve it." He gestured the bag at her again.

Despite not wanting to take the present, Kerri felt guilty that Jack had punched his best friend and took the bag. "I'm sorry too. I shouldn't have been so angry at you. And Jack shouldn't have hit you."

"We're cool. I get it. I have to go, more stops to make. Have a nice holiday, Kerri."

She pulled the tissue paper out of the bag to reveal a copy of Dangerous Minds on DVD. "Yeah, you too," Kerri shouted after him as he made his way down the driveway.

Dad plugged in the lights of the tree and called up the stairs for Kerri and Jack to join them to open presents on Christmas morning. Kerri seated herself on the floor in front of the couch while her dad handed out the gifts. Kerri was about to open one marked from Mom and Dad when the telephone rang. She leapt from the floor of the rec room and raced to the kitchen to answer.

She made it by the second ring and almost dropped the receiver as she rushed to pull it from the hook. Her mother was close behind, "it's awful early for a telephone call, especially on Christmas." Eileen made her way to the coffee perk. "Who is it?" She whispered at Kerri.

Kerri ignored the question and stretched the phone cord across the room, sitting herself at the dining room table with her feet above her, against the wall. Eileen nodded, she had seen this position before, Kerri was talking to Summer. She gave her daughter a little smile and left to give her privacy, hoping this chat would be exactly what Kerri needed to start feeling better.

"So, how have your holidays been so far?" Kerri twirled the phone cord in her fingers.

"You know, family and stuff, but it has been nice to see my old friends again. I would much rather be there with you."

***

Kerri could picture Summer as she was talking. There were many nights the two had sat facing their bedroom windows and talking for hours on the phone. "I know what you mean. Everyone just keeps asking me if I'm okay, it really sucks. I just wish they could mind their own business; you know?"

"Well I guess I shouldn't ask you if you are doing alright? There has to be a reason they are asking. They care about you."

"I suppose, and I guess I have been a little quiet around here lately. But I just have a lot on my mind."

"Anything you wanna talk to me about?" Summer's voice sounded almost pleading as she spoke. She hadn't been sleeping well either. She had talked her parents into letting her make this phone call with the sole purpose of making sure things were alright with Kerri.

"Are we alright? I mean, I know it was kinda weird with us when you left. Can we just forget everything that happened and be friends, like before?" Kerri had planned her words carefully over the week and a half since they spoke last.

There was a long pause before Summer replied. "I don't want to forget about it." Summer had also had a lot of time to think about things. She thought the awkwardness was her fault because of the way she had practically pushed Kerri away when they got home that night.

"So, you are still mad. Why did you bother to call then?" Kerri's heart sunk. She had talked herself into believing this could all be forgotten, and they would be best friends again. But Summer had called, and that said a lot.

"Mad? What would I be mad about? Look, just know that I'm thinking about everything and that we will talk this out when I get home." Summer covered the phone and shouted into the other room. "I have to go; breakfast is on the table. See you in five days."

"Right, five days. See you then." Kerri hung up the phone and sat staring at the calendar on the wall. She would be home on Saturday.

Kerri bottled her anxiousness and excitement as she went back to the living room to continue to open presents with her family. Her father had done exceptionally well selling insurance this year and her parents decided to get her an expensive new camera as a gift.

She had never been more overjoyed with a present. The camera was fully manual with two extra lenses. She excused herself and headed to her bedroom to read through the instructions and get acquainted with the device. She had always loved photography and couldn't wait to see what this camera could do.

Over the next week she did nothing but take pictures. She took shots of her family, the cars driving down the street, the birds in the backyard and anything else that caught her eye. The camera became her source of happiness as well as a distraction from her feelings and what might happen when Summer returned. The phone call had helped to reassure her that it was going to be okay, but she couldn't help but think about the worst-case scenario when they actually had to talk about it all.

Kerri woke early on the Saturday morning Summer was to arrive home, hardly able to contain her excitement and almost shaking thinking about seeing her again. She bounded out of bed, threw on the jeans and sweatshirt she had been wearing the night before and ran down over the stairs, only pausing to grab her camera on the way out the door.

Kerri could hardly wait to point the lens at Summer. When she closed her eyes, she could see Summer in quiet pensive moments and knew photos of those moments would be like capturing a part of her soul on film. She sat on the front porch swing for close to an hour, snapping the shutter on occasion at a kid passing by on a bike and the way the tree limbs were reflected in the front window. She was beginning to feel a chill and contemplated going back inside when she saw the Donnelly's car heading up the road.

Kerri's excitement was building the closer the car came. She felt a rush of heat flushing her face when it finally came to a stop in the driveway. The back door swung open and Summer emerged. Kerri immediately noticed that her raven hair which had previously hung long, halfway down her back was now cropped just above the shoulders.

***

Summer's gaze flicked to Kerri's house and their eyes

met. She ran across the front lawn and the girls fell into an embrace. Kerri gripped Summer as though she thought she would never see her again. They spent the afternoon just sitting in the swing, small talking and chit chatting about the vacation, both wanting to say something, but neither knowing how to bring up what they were both thinking about.

The tension was like a glass fixture between them; see through, yet obviously there. Kerri knew that it was all because of one foolish statement she made in a moment of vulnerability and if Summer couldn't push the memory of that conversation from her mind, things would never be the same. Kerri frowned, she knew they needed to talk things out and she had promised they would when Summer got home.

She wanted to puke. The knot which had started in her throat had worked its way into her stomach. Her heart was racing as she tried to find the words to explain to Summer why the whole thing was best forgotten. She had tried to plan it out that morning as she waited, but any reasons she came up with sounded forced and silly.

Fortunately for her, it was Summer who finally broke the silence to bring it up. "Ker, I know you want to forget the whole night of the Gala, but I can't. I've been thinking about what you said since I made it home that night."

Summer took a deep breath, concentrating on what she was trying to say. Kerri licked her lips, and then chewed on the bottom one slightly. She was afraid of what was to come.

"I care about you more than anyone else and I really don't know what I would do without you. But, Kerri... I'm so afraid." Summer raised her voice a little more with each word. "For Christ sake, you won't even explain to me what you really meant that night. I'm going crazy guessing and second guessing."

Kerri's voice was choked with tears. "I just don't think I did the right thing by saying anything to you about how I feel."

Summer jumped in quickly, "Feel? So, nothing has changed after the way I acted when we got home that night?"

"Of course not. What do you mean, how you acted? I'm the one who treated you so badly, running out of the bathroom and not talking about this when we got back here. I just didn't want you to hate me."

Kerri glanced up at the window to find her mother peering out between the curtains. "Ah, I'm getting a little cold, can we continue this inside?" She motioned to the window so Summer would see where her mother was standing.

"Sure, let's go upstairs where we won't be disturbed." Summer grabbed Kerri by the hand, but Kerri shook her grip loose as they entered the house.

"Hi girls. Did you have a good time on your holiday Summer?" Eileen smiled at the pair.

"Pretty good Mrs. Walters. But I'm certainly glad to be home." Summer smiled back at her, before continuing up the stairs behind Kerri.

"Can I get you girls a snack or some hot chocolate?"

Kerri was rushing Summer up over the stairs and away from her mother's prying eyes. "No thanks, Mom. Maybe later on."

Summer opened the door of the room and flopped herself down in her usual spot on the bed. She was tracing the lines on the bedspread, unsure what to say next. Kerri started fiddling with the stock of film on her desk.

"Ker, can I ask you something?" She looked up from the bedspread but couldn't catch Kerri's eye. "When did you know?"

Kerri breathed deeply, composing herself, but also searching for the appropriate response to Summer's vague question. "I would say it was the first day you moved in. From the first time I set eyes on you I could tell there was something special about you."

"Not before?" Said Summer, surprised by the answer. She had wondered a couple of times throughout her teen years but couldn't allow herself to admit there was anything different about her.

"Before? Huh?" Kerri's voice trailed off. She forced her gaze upward and into Summer's eyes.

"I mean, I've wondered it too, but I just figured I hadn't met the right boy."

Kerri swallowed hard. "Would you believe me if I told you I think I've always known? I knew there was something different. I didn't have any interest in dating, but I never put it together, really."

"Always? Oh, Kerri, I'm so confused." Summer reached out and took Kerri by the hand pulling her closer to the bed in the rolling desk chair. She was focused on her thumb as it gently stroked the back of Kerri's hand and across her wrist.

Kerri took her other hand and started to softly run her fingernails along the side of Summer's forearm, watching as goose bumps formed and the hairs began to stand on end. Summer suddenly pulled her hand away and sat more upright on the bed.

"Have you done this before, told anyone this before?" Summer's eyes shifted back to the blanket design, unable to look at Kerri for the response.

"No. I ah, guess I didn't see any reason until I met you." Kerri cleared her throat and shifted over to the bed beside her. "I never felt like this." She closed her eyes and grabbed both of Summer's hands in her own.

"I think I'm ready. I think I want to be with you. No, that's not true." Summer shook her head, focusing her thoughts, "I can't stop thinking about it. I know I do." Summer could feel her body shaking. She pulled her hands away from Kerri, running them through her hair to push it out of her face before she spoke. "Just tell me you'll never break my heart. Cause if you do, I'll lose my best friend too." Her fingers ran absentmindedly over the patterns now as she focused her attention on the window.

"Summer," She turned to look at Kerri, who placed her hand lightly against Summer's face, "Are you sure about this?" Kerri jumped suddenly from the rolling chair and began to pace back and forth. "Cause once things change between us, there's no going back and I don't know if I can handle that."

Summer stood up and positioned herself in Kerri's path. As she approached, Summer slipped her hands over the Kerri's shoulders, brushing her fingers lightly through her hair. Kerri stopped in her tracks, focused only on the ocean blue eyes of the girl before her. She opened her mouth to speak but Summer swiftly placed her finger against her lips, yearning to hold on to the moment.

Kerri pressed her forehead into Summer's, and slid her hands up over her biceps, laying one on her shoulder and using the other to gently caress her face. Summer hooked her finger under Kerri's chin and pulled her up, eye to eye. She could feel the intensity crawling beneath her skin.

There was a quick tap at the door as it swung open and

the girls scrambled back on the bed, trying to act naturally. Eileen entered carrying a TV tray with hot chocolate and popcorn. She placed the tray on the desk and found a spot to sit at the end of the bed, turning to face the girls.

"You know girls, I'm really glad you found each other. I used to really worry about Kerri here but that was before you came along Summer." She patted Summer on the knee as she spoke.

"Yeah, I'm really glad too, Mrs. Walters." She couldn't help but smile at Kerri, who seemed to be in a deep panic after the close call.

"Will you be staying the night honey?"

"I'm not sure yet, it's been a really long day."

"Alright, but know you are always welcome. Have fun girls." Eileen closed the door behind her.

CHAPTER 4

From the moment they admitted their feelings, things changed between the two, even in the way they spoke to each other. The confession opened a door for them to talk about things they had never spoken to anyone about before. Kerri and Summer spent the rest of Saturday sharing everything and promised each other they would never keep secrets again. Kerri felt closer to Summer than she ever had to anyone. It was a new year and Kerri was becoming a new person.

She wanted nothing more than time alone with Summer to see where things would have gone before her mother interrupted. Summer knocked on the door of her room just after lunch the following day. She shifted nervously in the doorway, "Should I have called first?"

Kerri smiled, "No, of course not. Come in."

Summer closed the door behind her and sat in the desk chair across from Kerri on the bed. Kerri hung her legs over the edge of the bed and placed her hand on Summer's. "I'm free for the day." Summer threw her bookbag onto the bed beside Kerri. "I brought some old magazines and a couple of movies. I thought you might want to hang out?" Summer watched as Kerri ran her fingers over her palm and wrist.

"Always." Kerri pulled her hand away to tuck a piece

of Summer's hair back behind her ear.

Summer shivered at the touch and focused on Kerri who was shifting her gaze between Summer's eyes and lips, her hand still on the side of Summer's face where she had moved the hair. Kerri inched forward until she could feel Summer's breath on her face and closed her eyes. A quick rap at the door sent Summer rolling backward, slamming the back of the chair into the desk.

"Every time!" Kerri exclaimed as Jack barreled through the door and threw himself on the bed. "What the hell do you want?" She shot at him.

"Wanted to see if I could watch a movie with you guys? I'm bored." Jack picked up one of the magazines from the stack and started flipping through the pages. "And I also wanted to know if you guys could give me some advice, you know, about Martha?"

Kerri shrugged her shoulders at Summer. She couldn't turn her brother away if he wanted to talk about a girl, no matter how much she wished he would leave. Summer nodded in agreement. Kerri's thoughts drifted back, another perfect moment and another interruption. She was starting to think they would never kiss.

"Well, get on with it then. You must be desperate to come to me for advice about a girl."

"You know that's not true, Ker. I have come to you lots of times."

"Yeah, but usually about what shirt to wear on your date, or about whether you should break up with the girl before, or after her birthday." Kerri paused, "Please tell me you aren't going to break up with Martha! I thought you really liked her!"

"No, no. It's not that. More the opposite of that really. I do really like her, and that's the problem. I've never felt like this before and I'm not sure what I'm supposed to do next." Jack slid up next to Kerri on the bed, leaning against the headboard.

"Have you told her how you feel?" Summer piped up, suddenly wanting to be involved in the conversation.

"Well, not in so many words, but I did bring her flowers for no reason the other day. And I asked her to that special dinner last week where I thought I was going to give her my school ring, but she hated the restaurant and was so hung up on the fact that it was expensive that it felt like the wrong time." Jack shook his head, "should I have done it anyway?"

"You were going to give her your ring? This is serious." Kerri scratched her chin and Summer smiled when she saw the idea pop into Kerri's eyes. "Where did you go on your first date?"

"Bill's. She got a chocolate shake and a vanilla shake and asked for two extra cups so she could mix them together." Jack's face lit up as he spoke, "she told me the chocolate was too chocolaty and the vanilla was too vanilla so the best was to have half and half."

"Why didn't she just ask them to make it that way?" Summer jumped in.

"You know, I didn't ask."

"Anyway," Kerri continued, "Why don't you take her back to that spot and give it to her there?"

"That's a great idea!" Summer exclaimed.

"Damn right it is. I know I would love that kind of a gesture and I'm sure she will too."

"Well, you girls would know best." Jack picked up the VCR remote and fluffed up the pillow behind him. "That's exactly what I'll do. Now, what are we watching?"

***

On Monday when classes started again Summer had to face Phil for the first time since the Gala. He approached her the second she sat down in their shared Law class for an explanation as to why she wouldn't at least return his phone calls. The professor entered before she was forced to answer, and Summer ducked out of the room as fast as she could at the end of the hour to avoid him. It was noon when he finally managed to catch up to her in the hall.

"Summer, come on now, you could have at least called me back. You know I'm sorry, I just figured, you know, one drink wasn't going to make you notice."

"Screw you Phil, you know that is not how it happened. Besides, you promised me you weren't going to." Summer turned and started to walk away from him.

"Well... Well..." Phil ran to catch up to her and grabbed her by the arm. "Give me another chance. C'mon, I know I was stupid, I'm an idiot. What do you want me to say? Go out with me. Friday night?"

Summer sighed and shook her head at him. "Forget it. Not interested. What do you want me to say?" She pushed his hand off her arm and headed toward the cafeteria.

Kerri emerged from around the corner just in time to see the scene. "Hey there. I guess the girl can handle herself." She threw her arm over Summer's shoulders.

Summer chuckled, "damn right I can. You don't ever have to worry about me." She slipped her arm around Kerri's waist and the two headed off down the hall.

For one reason or another, they were surrounded by people that entire week. Kerri started to believe they would never get another moment alone and she wasn't sure she even had the nerve to make a move if they did. Her luck changed when Friday rolled around and it seemed they would have the house to themselves for the evening.

Jack had plans with Martha for the night and her parents were attending an anniversary party for Eileen's boss, leaving Kerri home alone. She and Summer always spent

Friday evenings watching movies in her rec room and this was Kerri's chance to make it a movie night that neither would soon forget.

That afternoon Kerri met Summer in front of the English building, just like every other day. Summer smiled ear to ear when she saw her approaching. These had become Kerri's favourite moments, as even the way they looked at each other, the way Summer looked at her now felt different. Summer laughed nervously while Kerri recounted a funny story from her day as they walked and before they knew it, they had arrived at their identical two storey homes. Kerri climbed the steps of the porch and paused to watch as Summer unlocked her door and headed inside. Just a couple of hours to go before they would get to be alone.

"Hey Mom!" Kerri shouted before running up over the stairs to try to decide on an outfit for the evening. She pulled every t-shirt she owned from the drawer, finally finding one of her favourite polos near the bottom. She hastily shoved the rest of the shirts back in the drawer and changed, examining her choice in the mirror. The sound of her mother's voice echoing a call of 'dinner time' up the stairwell brought her back to reality. She raced down over the stairs and plunked herself in her usual spot at the head of the table.

Jack was already seated and her father, who was making his way in from the rec room had nearly been knocked down with the force as she breezed by him. Jack started loading his plate with potatoes, getting most of it on the table in the process.

"So, Ker, doing anything tonight or what? I think Davey finally worked up the nerve to ask for another shot." Jack chuckled, "I mean, he is pretty relentless in trying to get you to like him. I kinda get the feeling you are never going to, though."

"Nothing really on the go for tonight. Me and Summer are just going to watch some movies and hang out." She bowed her head slightly as she spoke, not wanting to make eye contact with anyone. She was afraid that her true plans for the evening were written all over her face.

"In the meantime, Jack, do me and Davey a favour? Tell him to forget about it. I mean, he could have lots of girls, why is he so hung up on chasing after me?"

Jack just laughed. He was now more interested in his dinner than the conversation. Eileen jumped in. "But Kerri, honey, Davey is such a nice boy and he has been following after you since you were a little girl. Why don't you just give the poor boy an opportunity to make up for whatever went wrong at the Gala?"

Eileen had also hoped to get some tidbit of information about what had caused the fight between Jack and Davey. She knew it had something to do with his baby sister, but he wouldn't tell her what had happened, and Kerri was keeping her mouth shut about it too.

Kerri shook her head, playing with the food on her plate. "Mom, just forget about it, alright? I'm never going to get together with Davey, no matter how much everyone else seems to think he is the right one for me, I don't alright?" She glared at her mother.

"Okay, honey. It was just a suggestion, but if you really don't want to, that's up to you."

Jack dropped his fork at the outburst, a smirk crossing his lips. "Who is he?"

Kerri was confused by his out of nowhere remark. "Who is who?"

"The guy you like. You never get this upset about someone suggesting that you and Davey belong together, so the way I figure it, there has to be someone else. So, tell me, who is it?"

Kerri blushed at the accusation. "Screw off, Jack. There is no other guy."

She continued to avert her eyes from her brother. Although she hadn't really lied, there was no other guy, it was a lie all the same. Kerri quietly went back to her food, letting her mind wander to her plans with Summer later that evening.

"So Jack, big date with Martha tonight?" Jim's voice boomed across the table, breaking the uncomfortable silence created by Kerri's outburst at her brother.

"S'pose so. I think we're just going out for shakes at Bill's downtown. But, Dad... I was wondering..."

"Yes, son. You can borrow my car. But on one condition." Jim pointed his finger across the table at him.

"Anything, name it." Jack jumped at the chance to borrow the car without a lecture on getting older and needing to get a job so he could get his own.

"You have to take your mother and I to and from the party."

"No sweat, Dad. So, what time does that thing get underway anyways?"

Kerri had stopped paying attention entirely by this point. Despite all her efforts, she couldn't get Summer off her mind. She excused herself from the table, barely having touched her food and headed to her room.

Kerri had a lot of work to do that evening, but she couldn't help but focus her attention on the open blind in the window across the yard. She continued to flicker her eyes in its direction for more than an hour before Summer appeared in her room.

Kerri smiled, simply at the sight of Summer as she flipped her raven hair up into a ponytail before flopping down on the bed. A tremble extended its way down into her bones just thinking about kissing her, touching her or having her near. Although Kerri would call herself a passionate person when it came to her beliefs and opinions, she had never felt that passion so focused before.

She lifted her eyes from her book to see Summer picking up the phone in her room, and with a shudder of hope she waited to see if the line would ring on her end. She could see Summer talking to someone and was a little upset it wasn't her, but not overly hurt. Maybe a little confused as to who she was talking to.

Summer had seemed so troubled at dinner that evening her mother had suggested she call her best friend from back home. She really needed someone to talk to and for the first time since moving there, she realized it couldn't be Kerri. A slight smile crossed her face when Lynn picked up. Summer had already decided she was going to tell Lynn about this 'guy' she was confused about. The most difficult part of the whole situation for Summer was that it wasn't about a guy.

She made small talk with Lynn before trying to bring up the issue. "I'm just so confused about the whole thing. I mean, I really like them, but it would just make everything so complicated."

"Well, is he cute? Cause if he is cute and you really like him, I don't see what is so complicated about it." Lynn had always been Summer's sounding board at home. But their relationship was nothing like the one she shared with Kerri.

Summer started to feel like the only way she could explain her problem was to tell Lynn the whole truth of the matter, but she was so afraid of how she would react. The words didn't exactly come easily for her, but she somehow managed to blurt it out. "God, it's just so complicated because it's not just some guy."

"A special guy, is he? I bet it's that one that lives next door." Summer almost laughed out loud.

"Not quite but close. It's the girl that lives next door." The phone went silent and Summer could feel a lump in her throat start to choke her as she waited for Lynn to speak.

After a minute of silence, a small voice finally came over the line, "Ha, ha, very funny Sum. You actually had me going for a minute there, the girl next door! This from the girl who had her pick of the football team starting line last year! So, tell me the truth now. What is he like?"

Summer felt the tears welling up in her eyes. She tried to hold back the sobs as she continued. "Lynn, I'm serious. I can't explain to you what happened. All I know is she's perfect. In every way possible, perfect. I've never met anyone like her before and I just realized that it doesn't matter."

"What do you mean it doesn't matter?" Lynn's voice was more hurried now.

"I mean, what made it most confusing was wondering how people were going to react to me, and what the world would think of our relationship. But it doesn't matter anymore. I don't care what you think, or what anyone else does for that matter. Kerri is it for me. She is the only person I want to be with."

"C'mon now Sum, what are you saying? Are you calling me to tell me you're interested in women?"

"I hadn't meant to, but if you can't accept that, it'll be alright." Summer breathed a sigh of relief at having told someone how she was feeling.

"You're my best friend, Summer. This doesn't change anything. I'm sorry if I don't know the right thing to say, but you seem happier than I have ever known you to be and that is the most important thing."

Summer sighed in relief. She had been expecting a much worse reaction from Lynn, but they had been friends since they started school and she knew if anyone could be alright with this it was her. "Thanks for understanding. I was almost sure you would just hang up in my face if I told you the truth."

"Never. I'm always going to be here for you." Lynn's voice trailed off.

"I'm still really scared. What if people looking at us does matter?"

"It will only matter if you let it."

Summer could hear her mother calling her. She opened the door and shouted a response down the hall. "Lynn, I gotta go. Mom says I'm costing her a fortune. Can I call you next week?"

"Of course, you can. I want to hear all about this perfect girl."

Kerri stood in the window watching as Summer placed the handset back in the cradle and bounced back onto the bed. Summer smiled from ear to ear, and Kerri couldn't help but do the same. Nothing made her happier than Summer's smile.

It was a flurry of activity at the Walters home. Jack was hogging the bathroom as he got ready for his date and Eileen and Jim were rushing around trying to get dressed for the party. Kerri was starting to get impatient with Jack who had been in the shower for more than half an hour.

She banged loudly on the door. "There isn't enough water in the whole town for you to get clean Jack Walters." She banged at the door again. "C'mon, the rest of us need to get in there too!"

He didn't reply, but a minute later the water stopped, and she could hear Jack using his electric razor. Kerri leaned her back against the door and slid to the floor. The door opened behind her and she practically fell into the room as Jack headed down the hall in his towel.

"'Bout time." She stood and brushed herself off and began to close the door.

Jack shouted after her down the hall, "Jeez, you wouldn't know but you were the one with a date tonight."

Kerri could hear his laughter drifting down the hall as she pushed the door shut. She looked in the mirror, unhappy with the way her hair was falling that evening and even less happy about the freckles which seemed more pronounced than ever on her nose. She shook off the insecurity and finished getting herself cleaned up.

Kerri hit the bottom of the stairs just as her father was helping her mother into her coat. She couldn't help but notice how beautiful her mother looked in her dress and pearls. Eileen hugged her daughter quickly and left for the car. Jim paused to give some last-minute instructions.

"Now, don't forget to lock the door..."

"I know dad. Don't worry so much, would you?" She kissed him lightly on the cheek and straightened out his shirt collar. "Have a good time tonight, will you be out late?"

"Fairly, but you don't have to wait up. Have fun tonight."

Finally, the house was empty, and Kerri could concentrate on Summer's arrival. She tidied the rec room a bit and placed the DVD in the machine before gathering up the snack foods from the kitchen.

Kerri looked around and smiled. Everything was perfect. This night was going to be perfect.

CHAPTER 5

The days went by in a blur for Kerri, going to class and looking for ways to steal secret kisses with Summer, in bathroom stalls while they were at the college or during the few moments they got to be alone when they returned home after class. When Kerri had free time that she couldn't spend with Summer, she spent it with her camera. She had big plans for a photo project she wanted to work on while Summer was spending Easter with her grandparents.

"I think you are going to bankrupt me in film development costs." Jim yelled at Kerri as she ran down over the steps, camera slung around her neck.

Kerri laughed, "It would be a lot cheaper if I could develop it myself! Plus, you have been talking about finishing the basement..." Kerri prodded.

"Your stuff is really good, you know. Even if that is coming from dear old Dad. Perhaps we could talk about putting in a small dark room."

"You would really do that?" Kerri pleaded.

"We can start work on it together in the spring." Jim smiled.

Kerri placed a quick kiss on the top of her father's head and ran out the door to explore the wooded area behind the houses. Beyond their back gardens, the woods stretched for several kilometers with a number of ruts and gorges as well as a small stream. Kerri and Jack had spent many afternoons playing Hide and Seek or Cops and Robbers in the area when they were younger.

Just a few minutes into her trek, Kerri spotted an old fort hastily thrown together with pieces of scrap 2x4 and plywood. She and Jack had stolen the tools and materials from her father's shed to build their secret hideout the summer before Jack went to high school. She made him promise they would never tell anyone where it was, and he hadn't.

They spent almost the entire summer building it. The scraps of lumber were the left-over pieces from her father extending the fence that now separated the back yard between their house and Summer's. She wasn't sure where they got the plywood but, looking back, she could see her father bringing it home with the intention of letting his kids take it. Kerri and Jack spent more than a week lugging the supplies into the area and another week planning how to frame it up.

Kerri snapped a few shots from the outside where the paint they had hastily thrown on was now peeling and moss was beginning to grow in the small gaps between the boards. She entered through a small doorway, no more than four feet high and laughed as she remembered how much trouble they had trying to give the place a roof.

The floor was mostly rotting leaves and there were piles of snow built up in the corners. Kerri kicked through the leaves and dirt, sending an old Frisbee flying into the wall. There were gaping holes in the ceiling and the only other opening was the door. Kerri promised herself in that moment that someday she would build an actual cabin where she could escape from the world.

She lay on her back, taking photos of the clouds through the breaks in the ceiling and shivered when the wind picked up and whistled through the poorly constructed walls. It was starting to get cold and Kerri could no longer ignore the pangs of hunger she was feeling. She took one last shot of the hideout and started to jog back through the woods to get home.

Kerri wrapped her arms around herself as she jogged, wishing she had taken a jacket. It was a mild spring day when she left the house, so she chose only a vest to throw on over her sweatshirt. She regretted that choice as the wind continued to blow through the trees and cut to her skin.

As Kerri neared the edge of the woods, she broke into a run, trying to stave off the cold. She heard the crack of a tree branch to her right and turned to look when suddenly she was falling. Kerri screamed in pain as her body hit the ground. She had not only felt, but heard, a snap in her right knee and no matter how much she struggled, she couldn't get to her feet.

Kerri tried to turn over onto her back which sent another swell of pain through her leg. She could see black spots in her eyes and knew that she could pass out from the pain. Kerri could faintly hear her mother's voice in the distance, calling her father to come in from the garage for dinner. She yelled as loud as she could, but her mother either couldn't hear her from the distance or had already closed the door.

She had promised that she would be home for dinner, but there had been several occasions where she had lost track of time and didn't arrive. She'd at least had the good sense to inform her mother that she was headed to the woods. She had to hope that when she didn't show up for the meal someone would come looking for her.

Kerri was shivering harder and she wasn't sure if it was because of the cold or the pain. She was afraid of losing consciousness and started to sing any song she knew all the words to, anything she could think of that would keep her focused and awake. The pain from her knee was now spreading upward and she was sure she could feel it in her hip and her ribs as well. Kerri closed her eyes and gritted her teeth, trying to block it out.

She must have passed out, because when Kerri opened her eyes again it was getting dark and she could see the sun setting through the trees. She could feel the heat building in her leg and looked down to find that the jeans, which had hung baggy around her thighs, were now pulled tight against her leg. The swelling was getting worse and her teeth chattered as another rush of wind flowed over her body, deepening the cold.

Tears streamed down Kerri's face, she could no longer block out the pain or hold back the emotion. She started to wonder if she would die here, less than a hundred yards from her home. With that fear building she started to drag her body a little at a time towards the house.

Every pull sent more pain surging up through her leg. It took every ounce of will for her to continue and with every pull she used the pain to scream for someone, anyone, to help her. The trail she was leaving behind her body in the snow showed that she was making little progress, but she was determined to keep moving. Kerri battled her exhaustion, dug her hands into the snow and pulled her body forward again. Her hands were red and burned from the cold and her mind was slipping. Kerri screamed at the top of her lungs for her mother, anyone, to come looking for her.

Kerri dragged herself until her arms went numb. It was dark now, but she could make out the faint light from the back porch of her house cutting through the trees in the distance. Kerri closed her eyes and pulled once more sending another wash of pain up through her body. Her arms went limp and she allowed her body to relax as she passed out from the pain.

***

Eileen watched through the back window and hoped to see Kerri making her way through the trees. "Jim, I'm starting to get worried. Kerri said she would be home before this time."

Jim looked up from his newspaper, "I'm sure she's fine. Kerri's practically a grown woman. She probably just lost track of time. You know how she gets with that camera."

"I know, but she wouldn't be shooting after dark and her plan was to take the trail through the woods. You really think there is no reason for me to panic?"

"I'll bet she comes barreling through that door any minute." Jim gestured to the back door and went back to his paper.

Eileen paced the kitchen floor watching the minutes tick by on the clock on the stove until she could no longer see the back gate through the dark. "Jack!" She hollered up the stairs, "I need you to do something for me."

Jack bounded down the steps, stopping in front of Eileen in the kitchen. "What's up?"

"Put on your clothes, I want you to go look for your sister. You know all the places she would go back there."

Jack nodded as he shrugged on his coat and boots,

pausing only to grab a flashlight from the kitchen drawer on his way out. "I'm sure she's fine, Mom. I'll be back in a bit; she will be with me and you can give her a hard time for making you worry."

Jack was just a few minutes' walk from the gate when he saw a dark form lying in the snow. He felt his heart skip a beat as he realized it was his sister and rushed toward her. Kerri was lying unconscious and he slid onto his knees beside her, shaking her awake. Kerri opened her eyes slightly, "Jack..." her voice was weak. "I hurt my leg... you have to get some help. I'm so cold."

Kerri could see the look of panic on her brother's face. "Hang in there, little sis. I don't want to leave you, but I can't carry you. I'm going to go get Dad." He took off his jacket and covered it over Kerri's legs then pulled off his sweatshirt and wrapped it around her upper body.

Kerri struggled to keep conscious while she waited and pulled the clothing closer around herself, trying to soak up the warmth that had been left by Jack's body. She hummed her favourite Counting Crows song and listened closely for the sound of her father and Jack returning for her.

The snow she had packed around her knee had started to melt from the heat of the swelling, but it had relieved some of the pressure of her jeans digging into the flesh and lessened the pain a little. Kerri shivered again from the cold. The temperature had dropped five or six degrees since the sun went down, and even the extra warmth from the jacket wasn't really helping.

It seemed like an eternity before Kerri heard two sets of footsteps approaching. She sighed in relief when she saw her father's face through the trees. Jim put on a brave face and attempted a smile as he gently scooped her into his arms. Kerri winced as a new rush of pain washed through her leg with the movement. She finally relaxed a little as she wrapped her arms around her father's neck, feeling the warmth of his skin.

"Okay, honey. You just hold on. Everything is going to be okay."

Eileen was standing in the back doorway holding a quilt as Jim carried Kerri in through the back door. She threw the blanket over her daughter and grabbed the car keys from the kitchen table, following them through the house. Jim gently placed Kerri in the back seat of the car and headed for the hospital.

The next time Kerri opened her eyes she found herself in strange surroundings. She blinked a couple of times trying to focus her eyes and heard the beeping of monitors telling her she was in the hospital. She didn't remember arriving there, and for a brief moment she also forgot the reason that she was there to begin with. She couldn't forget for long as she tried to roll onto her side and felt the rush of pain as though someone has stabbed a knife through her leg.

She winced as her mother opened the door. "Hi honey. How are you feeling?" She moved across the room and sat on the edge of her bed.

Kerri was still a little confused. "Hi, Mom. I'm fine really. What's going on?"

Her mother sighed and took her hand, "you did quite a number on that knee of yours. The doctor says it's going to be a long time before everything is back to normal."

"Mom, when can I go home?" Kerri hated hospitals. There was just something about the way they smelled, and how the air tasted.

"Well, in just a little while they are going to have to

take you for a little surgery. Then they want to keep you for observation because you were unconscious when we brought you in." Eileen saw the look of shock spreading across Kerri's face as she realized the magnitude of the injury.

"It's no big deal they just have to fix it up a little on the inside and get rid of some of the fluid." Eileen brushed the bangs out of Kerri's face. They were always falling in her eyes.

"I don't want to have surgery. There has to be another way, something else they can do." Kerri stifled a sob. "I just want to go home."

"Now, now, honey. Everything is going to be just fine and you will be home in a couple of days." Eileen glanced back at the door. "Now, I have to go. The nurse will be here in a few minutes to get you ready. But first there is someone else that wants to see you." She kissed Kerri on the forehead before exiting the room.

Kerri closed her eyes and sighed. The door opened again, and Kerri could see Summer standing there. She was hesitant to cross the threshold and see her in that bed. Kerri stretched and pulled herself up so she was in more of a sitting position and smiled weakly. She was more than a little surprised to see Summer as she didn't expect her to be home until the following day. Kerri motioned for her to come over and sit next to her on the bed.

Summer slowly entered the room, jumping a little at the sound of the door as it banged closed behind her. She had arrived home from her grandparents early that afternoon and immediately made her way next door to see Kerri. She was greeted by Jack who was locking the door. He told her what had happened and that he was on his way back to the hospital.

Jack explained that they had spent the night waiting for news from the doctors, so he had offered to make a trip home to pick up clothes for Kerri and food for the rest of them. He also had to cancel his plans with Martha for the evening. Jack offered to take Summer with him to see Kerri and she jumped in the car.

Summer softly planted herself on the edge of the bed, scared to get too close and hurt Kerri's injured leg but longing to reach out and touch her to make sure she was okay. She reached over and gently brushed Kerri's bangs from her eyes. "I can't understand how it doesn't drive you crazy to have hair falling in your face all the time."

Kerri extended her arms to Summer. "Well, are you going to come here or not?" Summer leaned into her grasp and softly pressed her lips to Kerri's neck.

"I go away for one day..."

Kerri's laughter drowned out the rest of the sentence.

Summer tilted her head a little as she smiled. "What the hell happened?"

"Forget it, it was stupid. They're taking me for surgery soon, so we don't have a lot of time. Just tell me you will be here when I wake up?" Kerri grabbed hold of her hands.

The nurse entered the room soundlessly as Summer nodded and tried to steal a quick kiss. Realizing they were not aware of her presence, the nurse cleared her throat and turned quickly toward the door. "I'll just give you girls a few minutes."

Summer jumped up from the bed, feeling the blood rush to her face. Someone had seen them. She kept her eyes on Kerri who smiled and sighed. Whatever fear and anxiety Kerri had been feeling had melted away the moment their lips touched. The moment that Summer had walked through the door she knew that, no matter what happened, everything would be fine.

Kerri winked at Summer and turned to speak to the nurse. "No, no. I'm ready, might as well get this over with."

Summer left the room quickly at the first opportunity and found the rest of the Walters family waiting in the hallway. The nurse had seen them kiss. Her stomach rolled and she struggled to calm her breathing. They had been so careful not to get caught together that she started to feel like the rest of the world didn't exist when they were alone. She took a moment to collect herself before walking toward Kerri's family.

"How is she taking it? If there is one thing that girl is, it's stubborn." Eileen hugged Summer.

Summer struggled to get her words together. "She'll be fine. Did they tell you how long she is going to be in surgery?"

"Well, honey, they said about three hours and then they will be moving her to recovery. The nurse told us it would be best if we came back in the morning." Jim placed his arm over Summer's shoulders. "Why don't you get Jack to take you home? There is nothing you can do here. You can come back and visit tomorrow."

Summer nodded in agreement but had no intention of staying away until the following day. She had promised Kerri that she would be there when she woke from surgery and that was a promise that she planned to keep.

CHAPTER 6

Summer returned home just in time to sit and eat dinner with her parents. Her mother, Joan was clearing the plates when Summer finally spoke. "Kerri's in the hospital."

"Oh, my God. Is she okay? What happened?" Joan replied.

"She's going to be fine. She fell and hurt her knee. She should be coming out of surgery soon." Summer's head was down, staring at her dirty plate. "I was wondering if I could maybe borrow the car and go see her?"

"Sure honey, you can take me to work in the morning and go by then." Joan tapped her hand on Summer's shoulder.

"I meant tonight. I want to see her when she wakes up."

Joan smiled knowingly and let her shoulders fall, "I suppose that will be alright. Don't stay too long, Kerri will need her rest," She said as she handed her the keys.

Summer was advised at the nursing station that Kerri was in recovery and should be moved back to her room at any time. She paced the hallway rubbing her hands together nervously while she waited. It was only five minutes later when the gurney came rolling down the hall, being pushed by the same nurse that had caught them kissing.

Summer averted her eyes when she saw the woman and walked a little further down the hall to avoid having to speak to her. Once she believed Kerri was alone in her room, she made her way to the door and quietly pushed it open, peaking to see if Kerri was asleep.

"Hey, you," Kerri was still a little groggy from the anesthetic. "Well, I made it and they tell me I'm going to be as good as new."

Summer plopped herself on the bed near Kerri's head. "Well, of course you are. There is no one tougher than you."

Kerri reached up and gently brushed her fingers over Summer's cheek, smiling. "I don't know if I should tell you this, but I had some interesting dreams about you."

Summer blushed. She took Kerri's hand from the side of her face and softly kissed her wrist before interlacing their fingers and placing their hands in her lap where they could not be seen. They sat looking into one another's eyes and smiling for a minute until a tap at the door made Summer quickly drop Kerri's hand and come back to reality.

The nurse entered the room. "I didn't want to interrupt," she smiled. "Just need to give Kerri's IV one last check before my shift ends."

Summer could feel the beads of sweat on her lip and forehead as she watched the nurse work. "So, ah…" Summer's voice trailed off as she swallowed the lump in her throat. "Are you going to tell anyone?" She blurted out.

The nurse just smiled. "You're both adults. What you do is none of my business, and no one else's either, unless you want it to be." She placed a reassuring hand on Summer's shoulder.

Summer felt her muscles relax; she hadn't realized she

was so tense. Kerri chuckled a little and reached for Summer's hand. Summer could see the warmth in Kerri's eyes as she looked at her. She wasn't afraid but she could tell by her expression that Summer had been petrified. She tried to force a smile to reassure Kerri, but the tension was returning as she thought about how hard it was to keep their secret. Summer stayed, holding Kerri's hand until she went to sleep and then quietly shuffled out of the room.

It took almost a month for Kerri to be able to get around without help. She still had a full leg cast covering the repair on her knee but had thrown down the crutches a couple of days before, frustrated with her lack of independence.

Summer had been doting on Kerri since the accident, helping her to class even if it was on the other side of campus, carrying her books and bringing her lunch. "It feels weird. I think people are starting to stare at us." Summer whispered.

"I think you are being paranoid. They don't even notice us."

"Seems like people are whispering about us. Like, they stop talking when we come into a room and stuff."

Kerri just shook her head. "I know you are nervous and scared, but honestly, I don't think anyone has any idea about us. And they won't until you want them too."

Exams were just a couple of weeks away and it was only a week before Kerri would turn 19. She had been very clear with her parents and Summer that she didn't want some big thing made of it, but if the past was any indication, her mother wasn't going to listen. She had created a spectacle of her children's birthdays every year. Jack loved it but Kerri hated big crowds, especially when she was the one who had to be the centre of attention.

There were many hushed conversations in the days leading up to her birthday, some of which even included whispers between her mother and Summer when they thought she wasn't paying attention. Although she dreaded what was to come, it was sweet that Summer was involved, and it would all be over soon enough.

By Friday, it seemed all conversations stopped the second Kerri entered a room. Even Summer stopped talking to people on campus when she approached. If there was a surprise, Summer was really playing it up and even asked Kerri what she wanted to do for the occasion as they walked home that afternoon. Kerri just shrugged her shoulders. She had meant it when she said she didn't want to do anything.

"Come on, Ker, why don't we hit the matinee movie and then go out for dinner? You can't just sit around the house and sulk all day and all night." Summer grasped her forearm and turned Kerri to face her.

"I really just don't feel like celebrating. What's the big deal anyway?" Kerri was milking as much as she could out of the situation. She knew it was all a ploy to get her out of the house, but if Summer really wanted this, Kerri was going to make her work for it.

"But it's your birthday! And your nineteenth for that matter. We don't have to do dinner. We could grab a couple of drinks on campus, legally! We have to celebrate somehow. Whatever you want to do, just name it." Summer threw her arm around Kerri's shoulders and they continued their walk home.

"I know, I know. You all keep reminding me. I would really rather just find a way to spend some time alone. Just the two of us. We haven't managed to get more than five minutes together since I got hurt. Between my mother hovering all the time and your father still not working, we can't get a moment of peace." Kerri knew her pleading was a waste of time, but it couldn't hurt to remind Summer that she wanted more time with her.

Summer giggled nervously. She had wanted to plan a night in North Beach for them as Kerri's present, but Eileen had nixed that when she brought up the surprise party. "It will happen. But, let's get through making plans for tomorrow first. I say we should hit the Saturday afternoon double feature. They are doing a flash back to the 80s this week, The Goonies and The Princess Bride."

Kerri just shrugged. "Yeah, I suppose. I guess any time alone with you is better than nothing at all. At least it feels like we are alone in the theatre." As they reached the sidewalk outside their houses, she turned to face Summer and after a quick check to ensure no one was watching, slipped her finger into her front pocket and playfully shook Summer's hips.

Summer smiled again. "I should get inside. I need to get dinner started." She ran up the steps and into the house as Kerri watched from the sidewalk.

***

The double feature started at 1:00 pm the following afternoon and Summer arrived on the doorstep promptly at noon. That way they could walk the couple of blocks to the theatre and ensure they had plenty of time to grab popcorn and get the good seats in the back below the projection room.

Kerri waited for the lights to dim before reaching over and gently squeezing Summer's knee, grazing her fingertips up and down the top of her thigh. There were only a half a dozen other people in the theatre, and they had mostly chosen seats near the middle of the room. Summer reached her hand below Kerri's elbow and walked her fingertips down until she found the seam on Kerri's jeans. She hooked her nails into the edge and slowing rubbed the back of her fingers along Kerri's thigh.

Kerri's breath hitched as she tried not to make a sound to draw attention to them. They were barely through the opening scene of the movie when Kerri stood up suddenly, almost throwing her popcorn to the floor, after Summer had drifted her fingers just a little higher than she ever had before. Summer could feel the warmth and arousal radiating from Kerri's centre, even through the heavy denim of her jeans.

Kerri's face was flushed, as she pointed toward the washroom at the back and made her way there as quietly as possible. Summer waited a couple of minutes before following her. She closed the door softly behind herself and found Kerri facing her with a grin. "Well, someone either took that a little further than they meant to, or you are getting very brave, Ms. Donnelly." Kerri whispered.

Summer walked toward her confidently, grabbed her hand and led her into the stall at the back of the room, closing it behind them. "Just shut up and kiss me already, will you?"

Kerri pressed Summer's back against the door of the stall, pinning her arms to the cold metal and brushed her lips against Summer's clavicle. Kerri could feel the goose bumps forming on Summer's neck as she ran her tongue from her shoulder to just below her ear, then gently sucked on her earlobe. A quiet sigh escaped Summer's mouth as Kerri released her wrists and ran the back of her hands down over Summer's sides before sliding one finger along her stomach where her shirt did not quite meet the waist of her jeans.

Kerri could feel the throbbing between her thighs intensify as she looked into Summer's eyes and placed her finger a little lower on Summer's body, trailing behind her waist band and threatening to undo her button. Summer nodded in agreement before grabbing Kerri by the sides of the face and pulling her into a kiss.

Kerri swiftly popped the button open and began trailing her fingers over Summer's stomach once again, this time, just inside the band of her underwear. Summer let go of Kerri's face nibbling a little on her lower lip and reached down to gently cup Kerri between the thighs, gently stroking her fingers back and forth over the seam of her jeans.

Kerri gasped and ran her hand over to Summer's hip, slipping it down inside her underwear and on to her ass. "Is this okay?" She nervously asked Summer as she ran her hand forward.

Summer nodded repeatedly and leaned into Kerri's ear to whisper, "more than." She flicked Kerri's earlobe with her tongue and pulled her hand up Kerri's groin and then back down, slowly unzipping her baggy jeans. Kerri moaned as she used her free hand to pull Summer closer by the elastic of her underwear and grazed her hand along the flesh of her stomach before finding her fingers dampened by Summer's arousal.

Kerri could feel herself pulsating as she became more and more wet, just from touching Summer. Summer whimpered at the touch and gently stroked the front of Kerri's underwear with her fingertips before finding her way inside the clothing to mimic Kerri's actions.

"I'm not really sure what I'm doing..." Summer admitted.

"You're doing great," Kerri panted, "Don't stop."

Kerri grabbed the back of Summer's neck and kissed her hard as Summer moaned into her mouth, with the release of her body. Kerri was close behind, pushing her hand through Summer's hair as the wetness pooled in her palm. Summer pressed her harder into the wall of the stall and covered Kerri's mouth to keep her from being too loud.

Kerri's breathing all but stopped as she struggled to keep her knees from shaking and allowed Summer to support her weight as the throbbing between her thighs increased to a maximum point before, she felt the relief.

They stood there for a few moments longer, foreheads pressed together and exchanging soft kisses between deep inhales to slow their collective breathing. "That was…" Kerri was interrupted by Summer once again softly pressing her lips to Kerri's.

"Incredible…" Summer finished.

"Yeah, well, that's one word for it. There are so many others." Kerri ran her hands up Summer's back until she was holding her by the shoulders. "We should get out of here. Or, like, at least go back and watch the rest of the movies."

Summer nodded. "I'll go first. Wait a couple of minutes and I'll see you out there."

Kerri plopped back into her seat at one of her favourite parts of the movie and immediately started to laugh, reaching out to take Summer by the hand. The intensity of their touching was quelled for the moment and they exchanged shy smiles and hand squeezes without speaking through the rest of the double feature.

Summer noticed Kerri's mood changed slightly when they left the theatre, "Are you okay? You seem to be all up in your head right now. Is it about what happened?"

Kerri gave her a half smile before turning to face her and taking her by the hands. "That is a lot of questions. I'm amazing. I might have liked for that to happen anywhere but a bathroom stall, but that's not what it is. I know you are planning something for my birthday. You don't really think that all of the hushed conversations you have been having with my mom have gotten past me, do you?"

Summer looked up with as much of a shocked expression as she could muster. "Why would you think that we have been having hushed conversations about you?" She said, teasing.

"Okay, fine. You can try to lie to me, but I see right through you. You know that you can't keep things from me."

Summer noticed a car turning down their street and quickly dropped Kerri's hands and ran her thumbs behind her ears and her hand over her head to fix her hair. Summer was still on constant alert about people seeing them in any kind of affectionate moment. It was strange, really. Since the first day they met, they would often hold hands or put their arms around each other, but from the moment they had kissed she was terrified that people would read more into how they were touching. She worried that people would see that it meant something more.

"So, should I be ready to look surprised when I open the door? I'm okay if you guys did have something planned. As much as I hate parties, nothing could spoil my birthday now."

Summer nodded. "I guess we will see how good of an actor you are."

Kerri threw open the door as the lights flicked on and a room full of family and classmates yelled, "SURPRISE!"

She put on her best shocked face and winked at Summer, "How did I do?"

CHAPTER 7

Exam week kept them both busy and it was the Friday of Kerri's final exam of the semester before they were even able to make the walk home together. They exchanged knowing smiles as they walked, but neither bothered to even try to make small talk.

Kerri still had a slight limp from the knee injury. The doctors told her with time it would get better and she would hardly notice that anything had ever been wrong. She was skeptical about that but continued the prescribed exercises and hit the gym twice a week for the strength building portion of her rehab. Kerri was still thinking about her limp when she realized they had arrived at home. "Are you seeing what I'm seeing?"

Summer squinted her eyes and raised one eyebrow, "What are you seeing?"

"No car. I don't think anyone else is home." Kerri turned toward her front step and motioned with her head for Summer to follow her as she headed into the house.

"Mom? Dad? Jack? Anybody here?" Kerri shouted as they kicked off their shoes in the porch. "Seems we are all alone." Kerri licked her lips and pressed Summer gently back against the door into a quick kiss.

Kerri shuddered. Every time their lips met felt the

same as it had the very first time. "That just made my day." Kerri kissed her lightly again.

Summer slipped her hands around Kerri's face and gently down to her neck as she pulled her deeper into the kiss. Kerri's hands trembled as she brushed them around Summer's waist and hooked her fingers through the belt loops on the back on her jeans, pulling Summer's body closer.

The sound of footsteps on the stairs behind them pulled Kerri back to reality as she quickly moved away from Summer and turned to see her brother, frozen and staring at them. Jack had stopped mid-step, still holding the rail, mouth agape as he came around the corner to find someone kissing his sister in the front porch.

"I... ah... I'm sorry. I... ah... oh, God. I didn't mean to. I mean..." Jack's words awkwardly fell from his mouth as he struggled to make a sentence or put his thoughts in order. "I just, I mean, I had no idea you were here."

The lump in Kerri's throat continued to grow as she gasped for air and stared back at Jack, trying to determine exactly how much he saw. "I called out," she croaked. "I didn't think you were home." Kerri's vision was getting blurry as tears began to form.

Jack finally started to move, making his way slowly down the rest of the staircase. "Headphones. I had my headphones on. Wow, I mean...wow." Jack realized that he was still slack-jawed and staring at the two. He shook his head and looked back at them with a grin.

Kerri could feel her hands shaking, she wasn't sure how to ask what he had seen, and she really wasn't sure what his reaction meant. "Jack, I don't know what you think you just saw," she started, glancing back at Summer, "but it wasn't what you think."

Jack just chuckled. "I'm pretty sure what I saw was the two of you kissing. I'm not sure how that could be misunderstood as anything other than what it was." Jack thought for a moment, "Well, I guess that explains a lot."

Kerri could feel the heat of the tears as they steadily streamed down her face. They had been caught. There was no going back. "Oh, my God, Jack. Please. Please, tell me that you aren't going to say anything to anyone about this?" She rushed over to him as she begged.

Jack's eyes softened and he placed his hand on his sister's shoulder. "Maybe I should start over." He threw a quick smile at Summer who was still standing with her back pressed to the door. "Mom and Dad will be home soon, let's go upstairs and talk. All of us."

Kerri and Summer shared a nervous glance as they slowly headed up to Kerri's room, stepping in time, with Jack in the lead. The lump that was previously in Kerri's throat was now sitting firmly in her stomach and she knew she could throw up at any moment as she sat on the edge of the bed and Summer found a place beside her.

Jack paced the floor in front of the two, chewing on the top of his thumb and trying to put his thoughts in order. He took a breath and looked up as though he would begin before shaking his head a little and continuing to pace.

"Jesus, Jack, are you going to tell anyone or not?" Summer's face flushed as she started to feel a little panic settle in. "Just say something, anything already!"

"I won't say anything if you guys don't want me to. Just bear with me, this is a lot to take in. So," He stopped pacing and smiled excitedly at the girls, "are you together, together? Was this the first time it happened?" He turned to Kerri, "Does this mean you're gay?"

Kerri could hear her breath shaking as hard as her

hands were in her lap. She glanced over at Summer. He was asking them questions about things that they hadn't even defined for themselves. "This was not the first time, no. As for the rest, I don't know and I... I think so."

"Okay." Jack leaned his head between the two girls and gave them both a hug of reassurance. "I just want you to be happy. If she is who makes you happy, then I am all for it." He released the embrace and moved back from the bed. "I'll leave you alone to talk." Jack swiftly closed the door as he headed out of the room.

The lump in Kerri's stomach was starting to subside slightly and she could see relief flood Summer's face. Someone they knew had found out, and the world didn't come to an end. Kerri slid her hand over Summer's thigh and down to her knee. "I have been kinda wanting to bring this up with you, but I wasn't really sure what to say." Kerri focused her attention on the placement of her hand, "I was afraid that if I talked about it, this might get too real for you or it might scare you away." Kerri took a deep breath and looked into Summer's eyes, "Together, together?" She inquired to Summer and held her breath in anticipation of the answer.

"Kerri, I'm scared. If we put a label on what we are, does that mean you are going to want to tell other people? What does it mean for me? I'm not sure I'm ready to put a label on me. If we say we are together, does that mean I have to say I'm gay? Cause I don't know if that is true. I just know that I have feelings for you." Summer's mind raced.

Kerri straightened her shoulders and shifted to face Summer on the bed. "Whether we label it or not, you know that we are in a relationship. There's no denying it. Saying it doesn't have to change anything, but I would really like you to say it. I don't want to keep doing this, all the hiding, all the lies, if we are just fooling around. I love you. I think you love me too."

"Kerri, I just… We aren't just fooling around. I'm not just fooling around. I do love you, but I don't want to be this way. I thought I could handle it. I thought I could deal with the secrets, for you, I thought I could. But I don't want people to know either. I don't want them to look at me like I'm different. I don't want to them to stare or spend the rest of my life listening to the whispers."

"We don't have to tell anyone right away. I'll…I'll get my own place." Kerri got up from the bed and started to pace the floor of the bedroom. "We wouldn't have to worry about anyone coming in unexpected. We could take our time and see where this goes." Kerri almost pleaded for Summer to agree.

"I can't. I can't be this way." Summer felt the warmth as tears started to pour down her cheeks. "I want a home, and a family. I want to be normal. I can't do any of that with you."

Kerri fell to her knees in front of Summer, wrapping her arms around her legs and burying her face in her lap. "Please, please don't say that. I love you. I'm in love with you. I can give you all of those things, you just have to let me."

Summer stood from the bed and Kerri jumped to her feet to stand between her and the door. "Maybe we could just go back to being friends. It would be so much easier if we could just go back to being friends, like before." Summer's voice broke as she spoke, and she took Kerri's hands as she forced herself to continue. "It's not everything that you want it to be, but I want you to be a part of my life."

Kerri just shook her head and looked down at her feet.

Her panic changed to an empty feeling she had never experienced before. "And that is something I can't do. I need this to be more. If I can't be with you, then I can't have you in my life anymore. I can't want you like this and not be with you."

"The truth is I really thought I could do this. I even told my best friend from back home about you. That I thought I had feelings for you. That I do have feelings for you." Summer found herself blurting out everything that had brought them to this moment. "She was even okay about it and that made me think I could be with you and it would be alright."

"Then what in the hell has changed between then and now? It is because more people know? Jack said he wouldn't tell. We can tell people, or not tell people, whatever you want to do! Just don't do this to me. Come on, Sum, give us a chance. You know you want to be with me. You can't tell me different. I feel it every time we touch, every time we kiss." Kerri thought she could sense a little hope in Summer's confession that meant it might not be over after all.

"I do want to be with you and no it's not because more people know now, it's because people will keep finding out. I can't handle the names people will call me - call us! I saw it happen to this girl in my Gender Studies class a couple of days ago. There were people shouting dyke at her in the parking lot, guys yelling that they could change her mind. I just, I can't deal with that." Summer started to cry and pushed past Kerri, pausing in the doorway. "I want to be with you. I really do. And I love you, but I can't deal with any of this."

Kerri had barely understood the words Summer was saying before she heard the front door slam. Her legs betrayed her as she felt her body slump to the floor and she curled herself into a rocking position, not knowing how to stop the words from repeating over and over in her head.

Kerri wasn't sure how long Summer had been gone, or how long Jack had been standing in her doorway when she finally looked up at him. She released her arms from around her knees and slowly stretched her legs down to the floor, feeling the ache in the one she had injured. She wiped her face on the back of her hand, "Jack," she managed to croak. "It's over, Jack. I don't think I can breathe."

He dropped his body beside hers on the floor and wrapped an arm around her shoulders, but she shrugged him off. He crossed his legs in under himself and sat facing his sister. "Kerri, I'm so sorry. Is it my fault? I shouldn't have asked so many questions. I shouldn't have come downstairs earlier. I don't even know why I did." He tried again to reach out to her, but she pulled away.

"It's not your fault. I don't really understand what happened. Things were going so well." Kerri sobbed and took the hand he had extended to her. "I'm in love with her, Jack. Totally, completely in love and she says she can't be with me. She says it's too complicated, too hard."

Jack smiled a little. "I have never heard you talk like this about anyone. Maybe she will come around. Give her some time. I can't imagine what this is like for either of you, but I kinda figured about you for a while." He glanced around the room at some of the same items that had made Kerri question herself.

"What do you mean, you kinda figured?" Kerri swallowed back her tears and tried to collect herself.

"Well, there were a couple of signs. I mean, Martha's sister is gay and she has all of these same posters and most of the same CDs that you have been bringing home lately. And then there was the whole thing with Davey. You didn't act like any girl I have ever known who got that much attention from a guy." Jack slid himself along the hardwood so they were seated shoulder to shoulder. "Most girls would have at least led him on, you just seemed annoyed."

"I was annoyed. I didn't want his attention. He was like a stray cat that you just couldn't seem to get rid of because you fed it that one time. I never could understand why he wouldn't just give up and leave me alone."

Jack snickered. "Probably because you weren't like any of the other girls. He just didn't understand that it was because you were into the other girls." He leaned toward Kerri, knocking their shoulders together. "You did make me second guess myself when you agreed to go out with him, though."

Kerri tried to stifle a laugh. "Ha ha, Jack. Very funny. Do you think anyone else figures? I mean, do Mom and Dad…"

Jack straightened his shoulders and put on his most serious face. "Ker, I don't think anyone else has any indication. Mom and Dad definitely think that you have been acting a little strange lately. Mom asked me about it just the other day. But, strange in a positive way. She wondered why you were acting so happy all the time, and not brooding around the house like you used to."

"Hey! I was never broody!"

"Well, you were at least angsty. Always listening to angry girl music on blast with your door closed. The only time you smiled was when you were spending time with Summer. It's been so different since Christmas."

Kerri rocked side to side, letting their shoulders bump

a couple of times. "I never knew that I wasn't happy, until the moment that I realized I was. And in the same moment, that happiness was taken away from me. How do I make her change her mind?"

Jack put his arm around her and pulled her head down onto his shoulder. "I don't think you can. But I do think she will come around. Give her some space for a couple of days, then go talk to her." He tilted his head down on top of hers, "and no matter what happens, I'm going to be here for you, okay?"

Kerri wrapped her arms around his chest and fully gave in to her emotions, her shoulders shaking as she sobbed. "I know you will."

CHAPTER 8

Kerri took Jack's advice and tried to give Summer space. For three days she didn't call, didn't go to her house and barely left her own room in fear they would run into each other on the street. Kerri was bursting to talk to Summer, to ask her to reconsider, but she knew she had to give her time. Kerri planned the words she would say, carefully repeating them over and over to herself to make sure that her points were clear and calm.

Kerri could hardly sleep the third night, replaying her last conversation with Summer over in her head and waiting for the morning to come so she could call and ask Summer to give her another chance. Kerri looked through the window and watched for Summer to get out of bed, but when she hadn't moved by ten, she decided to pick up the phone anyway.

As the rings went through on the line, Kerri tried to keep herself calm, but the voice that finally answered was not Summer. "Mrs. Donnelly, would Summer be home?"

"Just a minute." Kerri waited and tried to make out the words coming from the muffled voices on the other side. Joan sighed, "I'm sorry, Kerri honey. Summer can't come to the phone right now. Should I tell her that you called?"

Kerri watched Summer move around her room and close the blinds. "Yeah, tell her I would really like to talk to her."

"Okay dear. I will."

Kerri hung up the receiver and paced around the room. She jumped in the shower and got dressed. If Summer wouldn't answer her calls, she would go over to the house instead. Kerri crushed her feet into her sneakers and stormed out of the house, down over the stoop and up onto the porch next door. She brushed her bang out of her eyes and checked that her shirt tail was properly tucked in before knocking.

Joan opened the door and gave Kerri an 'I'm sorry' look. "Hi honey. Summer is in her room, but she says she doesn't want to see you right now."

"Can I at least try to talk to her?"

"I'm afraid I can't let you come in. I'm not sure what you two are fighting about, but she's really upset. She won't tell me what is going on. Would you at least tell me what this is all about?"

Kerri scuffed her foot against the board on the porch. "It's not my place to tell you. If you want to know why we are fighting, you will have to get Summer to tell you. Please tell her that I came by?"

Joan nodded, "I will. I'm sure she will come around, whatever it is."

Kerri called for Summer every day for the next twelve days before Summer finally agreed to come to the phone. "Kerri, you have to stop calling. You're starting to seem crazy." Summer whisper shouted into the receiver.

"Please, why won't you even talk to me about this? We can work it out, I know we can, but you have to talk to me." Kerri hadn't meant to sound so needy, and even after practicing what she would say since Summer walked out of her room, she had immediately gone off script when she heard her voice on the other end of the phone.

"I said everything I need to say to you." Summer's voice started to break.

"Then why do you still sound so upset?" Kerri sighed. "Let me start this again. There is nothing that we can't handle, as long as we take it on together. I know people can be cruel, I know that there are others that will be supportive and protect us. I know that I have never felt as happy as I do when I am with you and I want to build a life with you."

"Listen to me, Ker. I can't be like you and I can't be with you. I still want you to be my best friend, but there is only one way that can happen. You have to let it go. Move on. Until you do, I don't want to talk to you or see you. Can you respect that?" Summer forced the words from her throat, trying to keep Kerri from knowing that she was crying.

"Fine, push me away. How about when you figure out how to be true to yourself, you give me a call?" Kerri banged the receiver into the cradle and ran up the stairs, slamming her bedroom door behind her. She cried into her pillow until she was completely exhausted and fell asleep.

Kerri's eyes popped open at the sound of her door opening. Eileen peeked around the corner, "Kerri? Are you awake?"

Kerri rolled to face her mother, blinking hard against the ache in her eyes from the hours that she had spent crying. "Yeah."

Eileen made her way to the bed to sit beside her. "Oh, honey. I wish you would tell me what's wrong. You've been moping around here for weeks. Did you and Summer have a fight? It's so strange that she hasn't been around."

Kerri just shook her head and fought to keep the tears from starting again. She was sure that if she started to cry the words would come flowing out as well. Her mind raced. She wanted to talk about it. She had always known that she could talk to her mother about anything, but she wasn't sure how she would react. Kerri didn't know if she could trust that her mom would be supportive, and she couldn't handle any more heartache.

Eileen gently rubbed Kerri's arm and took a deep breath. "The pain of first love doesn't last forever." She focused her attention on the rhythmic motion of her hand. "I've seen a big change in you over the past couple of months. You seem so happy, more than you ever have. I had been leaving you alone, I hoped that you would come and talk to me about it."

"How did you know?" Kerri's eyebrows raised in surprise.

"I figured it out around your birthday. I think I may have ruined Summer's plan when I told her about the surprise party I had in the works." Eileen brushed Kerri's bang out of her eyes. "You can tell me what happened if you want. I promise I will just listen."

Kerri buried her face in her mom's leg as she allowed the tears to fall. "I just don't know how to be okay anymore."

Eileen rubbed Kerri's back, hushing her sobs. "You will, honey. You will. As much as it hurts right now, and I know that you don't believe it to be true, but you will even love again. Do you want to tell me what happened?"

Kerri sat up in the bed and held her knees to her chest, recounting the whole story from the moment that her relationship with Summer changed. Eileen tried to keep smiling as she listened to Kerri sob though the words. She held her for a long time when she finished before speaking.

"Love is hard. It's complicated and confusing no matter who you fall in love with." She wiped a tear from Kerri's cheek. "I know this is not what you want to hear right now, but you will fall in love again, maybe many times. But what it sounds like to me, is that you can still keep your friend."

Kerri sniffed and wiped her face in the back of her hand. "I don't think I can. She won't even talk to me right now, and when I see her, I just want to beg her to try again. I want more than that and I don't know how to be around her if I can't have it."

Eileen smiled. "It might not happen right away for you, but you will move on and if you really want Summer in your life, you will find a way to be okay with just friends."

Kerri stared at her mother as she spoke. "Thanks." Eileen tilted her head in confusion at the pleasantry. "I mean, thanks for making this so easy, for not freaking out, you know?"

"Well honey, I like to think your father and I are at least a little bit liberal and open minded. We just want you to be happy. I don't care who you are with, as long as they can do that." Eileen brushed the tears from Kerri's cheek. "You are going to be okay and I will always be here for you."

Kerri nodded and bowed her head. "I know. I'd like to be alone for a while right now, if you don't mind."

Eileen squeezed her hand and stood from the bed. "Not at all. You get some rest." She gently closed the door behind her as she left.

Kerri spent most of her summer working on her photography. As promised, she and her father had taken almost a month converting part of the basement into a dark room, so on nice days she took her camera and walked around town, and when it rained, she spent her time developing the film. She even applied for a transfer into the Journalism program at Jenkinstown College in the fall and was accepted.

Kerri occasionally ran into Summer on her forays around the community and they would make small talk, but it was uncomfortable as Kerri was still fighting with herself not to beg Summer for another chance. More often than not, Kerri had taken to heading into the closest store when she saw Summer coming.

It was a week before classes started again when Kerri left the house to find Summer standing on the sidewalk, scuffing her foot and biting her lower lip. She stood frozen on the porch, knowing there was no way to avoid her. Kerri even thought about going back inside as though she had forgotten something, but before she could make up her mind, Summer was walking toward her.

"Hey." Summer offered a meek greeting.

"Hey," Kerri said confused. It had become so much easier to avoid Summer over the last couple of weeks that she assumed Summer was avoiding her too.

"So, I didn't want to just leave without saying anything." Summer bit her lower lip again, trying to gather the courage to go on. "I was going to tell you, and then I thought I shouldn't, but now I realize that I have to."

Kerri struggled to follow what she was trying to say. "I have no idea what you are talking about. You want to try that again?"

Summer swallowed hard. "After what happened, I had a really hard time. And, wait," She put up her hand to stop Kerri from interrupting, "I know that it was all my fault so please don't say anything yet." Summer's shoulders heaved as she inhaled sharply. "I didn't know if I would be able to face seeing you every day, so I applied for late acceptance at the University of North Beach..." She stopped scuffing her foot and looked up at Kerri. "I got in. I'm moving away."

"Why do you think I care?" Kerri knew that she shouldn't be, but she was angry at Summer for leaving.

"I don't know. I just, I really, I felt like I needed to tell you." Summer swallowed hard. "I used to tell you everything. I'm sorry that things got so messed up. But most of all, I'm sorry that I hurt you and then pushed you away." Tears began to form in Summer's eyes, but Kerri stood firm in her anger.

"Oh, you're sorry. Is that supposed to make me feel any better? You broke my heart. You did the one thing that you promised you wouldn't do, and I lost my best friend, just like I said I would. No amount of sorry can make any of this better." Kerri folder her arms across her chest, "and now, NOW, you are just going to up and move to North Beach, just to get away from me?"

"Please don't shout and make a scene." Summer choked, "I broke my heart, too."

Kerri quickly closed the distance between them and lowered her voice, pointed a finger in Summer's face and gritted her teeth together. "Not enough to make you try to work things out. Not enough for you to even listen to me when I tried to tell you that it didn't have to be this way. Not enough."

Summer raised her hands in surrender. "I'll go now. I just couldn't leave without coming to tell you. I will write to you, if you want."

"Do whatever you want to do. Just don't do me any favours. I hope you have a nice life." Kerri turned and quickly ran up the steps of the porch, entered the house and slammed the door behind her.

CHAPTER 9

After five years as a photographer with the Jenkin-stown Gazette, by the summer of 2007 Kerri was hungry to spread her wings and do something new. She was ready to get away from the small town where she had grown up and make a fresh start. At 26 years old, she had never lived further away from her parents than down the street with her brother just a block away.

Her desire to leave home wasn't helped by the fact that she was still single and there were not a lot of prospects around. Kerri's mother had been right when she said that she would find love again. She did. First with Jenny, who she met buying cough syrup at Jenkinstown Drugs. That lasted a grand total of six months before Kerri got restless and decided it was time to move on, mostly because of Savannah.

Kerri met Savannah at a press conference her first year out of journalism school. They agreed to meet for a drink at the end of the day and Kerri was smitten. She had really thought it could work between them and they were very happy for the first two years. Things started to go down-hill when Savannah started to talk seriously about their future. She was pressuring Kerri to settle down and start a family and Kerri just wasn't ready.

She made a lot of excuses as to why they should wait, and it started the rift between them. Kerri insisted that she had a five-year plan that would eventually see them settled down, but Savannah started to withdraw from the relationship. They stayed together for another year before Kerri finally admitted that she couldn't see the rest of her life with Savannah, so it had ended.

She hadn't dated anyone since the breakup almost eight months before and she was ready to start over somewhere new. Kerri was also looking to take the next step in her career, so it was perfect when she saw the opening for a photojournalist at the North Beach Observer. North Beach was a much larger place and would give her plenty of opportunities to show off her abilities and start fresh.

She carefully crafted a cover letter to attach to her CV and emailed it to Observer editor Steph Underwood. Kerri really liked the idea of working under a female editor as well. She had barely closed the internet window on her computer when her cell phone started to buzz on her desk.

"Kerri Walters," she said, answering a number she didn't recognize. Kerri grabbed her camera and started toward the door, phone pressed between her ear and her shoulder.

"Hi Kerri, Steph Underwood. How are you?"

Kerri juggled the phone and her camera in shock at the voice on the end of the line. "I'm doing well, how are you?"

"I just received your resume and I was hoping you would be interested in coming into the office for an interview tomorrow."

Kerri swallowed hard. "An interview? Tomorrow? Sure, yeah. I can be there."

"Excellent. We will see you then." Steph hung up the phone.

The second Kerri heard the click she sat back at her computer to start putting together a portfolio of her work, including several of the images that had garnered her award recognition over the years. The screen lit up, showing Kerri's Facebook page with several new friend requests. She had let Jack talk her into signing up for the new social media phenomenon over a couple of drinks the day before and was almost instantly regretting it. Half of the people that wanted to be her friend were people she hadn't spoken to since high school and the other half were colleagues she had worked with over the years, or people from college.

Jack had insisted, though. He was getting ready to move across the country with his wife, Martha, and their two kids, for Martha's new job and he told Kerri it would be a good way for them to keep up with each other's lives. She was skeptical but agreed to make a page for his sake.

Kerri clicked on the icon and started to read the names of the people that wanted to be her friends. Kerri sipped on her diet coke and almost choked when she saw Summer Donnelly-Peters. She felt the blood drain from her face and her chest tightened as she read the name again. She had often wondered what happened to Summer but having the answer right in front of her was overwhelming.

She clicked the link to see her profile and stared at the picture of Summer standing arm in arm with a man who was holding a baby in his other arm and smiling at the camera. Kerri's lungs wheezed. Peters. Summer was married, to the man in the photo. She was getting all the things that she had said Kerri couldn't give her. Kerri started to click through the other photos that Summer had posted, trying to decide if she wanted to accept her friend request.

There wasn't much to see, a photo of Summer at the beach and a graduation photo which Kerri assumed was when she finished University. Kerri struggled between accepting the request to be able to see more details of Summer's life, and being afraid to know the answers. She held the mouse over the accept button for a few minutes, breathing deep before finally clicking yes.

She was still in a bit of disbelief that she had agreed when she received a notification that someone had posted on her timeline. Kerri giggled a little at the prospect that the post might be from Summer, but her heart beating out of her chest said she was more anxious that it wasn't. Her hands were shaking as she moved the mouse to the icon to check.

Summer Donnelly-Peters > Kerri Walters
June 5, 2007 4:02pm
Hey there! It's been a long time! Thanks for accepting my friend request. How is life?

Kerri just sat in the chair staring at the screen, mouth agape. "A long time, yeah that's an understatement," she muttered under her breath. "How is life?" Kerri laughed then shouted at her computer screen. "You have to be kidding me. How is life. What does she expect me to say?"

She heard the door to the office click shut and blushed as she realized someone had overheard her exchange with the computer. Kerri tapped her fingers against the keys, trying to decide what to reply, or even if she should at all. Sure, she wanted to creep around and find out more, but she didn't want to have to hear from Summer about her life with this man and her baby. Kerri hadn't expected to be so upset over seeing Summer with someone else after so many years had passed, but she also hadn't really expected to see her at all.

Kerri Walters > Summer Donnelly-Peters
June 5, 2007 4:18pm
It has been a long time. Life is good. Job is good, family is good. Things, believe it or not, are kinda going according to plan. You?

It wasn't really a lie. She was about to interview for her dream job and her parents and Jack were doing well. Kerri hesitated for a long time, typing and back spacing, changing her mind over and over about whether she should do the courteous thing and ask about Summer. In the end, she decided it was only polite to ask if she was going to respond.

Summer Donnelly-Peters > Kerri Walters
June 5, 2007 4:20pm
That's great! I'm glad to hear that things are going well for you. My life is also good. I became a lawyer, after. I'm working as a public defender now. It's grueling, but really rewarding. As you probably noticed, I got married last year to one of the other lawyers in my office. We now have a little baby, Ava! She is just over three months.

Kerri swallowed hard and groaned. She shouldn't have asked. She gritted her teeth to give the response her mother would say she should.

Kerri Walters > Summer Donnelly-Peters
June 5, 2007 4:24pm
I'm happy for you. I'm a photojournalist. I've been working at the Jenkinstown Gazette since graduation, but it looks like I could be moving to North Beach before the end of the month. It was nice catching up!

Kerri had hoped that would be the end of that, but

a few minutes later she had yet another notification that someone had written on her page.

Summer Donnelly-Peters > Kerri Walters
June 5, 2007 4:27pm
It was! I actually live in North Beach. You should let me know when you come to town. I would love to meet up and actually have a chance to sit and chat. Really catch up on things.

Kerri started to panic. She would be moving to the same city as Summer. She could run into her by accident in the street or at the grocery store. It wasn't a very big city, big compared to Jenkinstown, but it wasn't New York or anything. There was even a chance they would see each other regularly with Kerri working for the newspaper and Summer being a lawyer. Kerri often covered high profile court cases.

Kerri closed her internet window and rubbed her hands over her face, brushing her bangs off her forehead. She gazed at her background photo long enough that her eyes started to blur. She couldn't reply again. The idea of maybe, possibly, on a rare occasion running into Summer was enough to make her sick, the thought of doing it on purpose made her weak.

She did decide to call Jack and see if he would meet her for a drink to talk about what she was including in her portfolio for her interview in the morning. Kerri was also hoping to slip in the information about her conversation with Summer. Jack had always been her sounding board when it came to the relationships in her life, starting with Summer.

She grabbed her cell phone from the desk, flipped it open and started to dial his number as she threw on her coat and headed for the office door. It was a few minutes earlier than she would normally head out. Even though it was Monday, it was the start of her weekend and she couldn't wait to talk to Jack.

He picked up on the first ring. "Hey big brother. What are you up to right now?" Kerri tried to force a smile. She had read somewhere once that it could make you sound happier.

"Oh, you know. Just playing around on Facebook… I see you have a new friend." Jack's tone was more serious that she had expected. "I'm thinking you are calling to ask me to meet you at Willie's for a drink."

"Damn. I forgot that all four of my other friends were going to be able to read that conversation. Yeah. I'm just grabbing a booth in the back. I'll order us some whiskey. Get here as soon as you can."

"Just give me 15 or so. And Kerri?" Jack's voice softened.

"Yeah?"

"Take a deep breath. You are going to be okay."

Kerri snapped her phone shut, ending the call just as the bartender greeted her. "The usual, kid?"

Kerri smiled. One thing that she would miss if she moved to North Beach would surely be her favourite bar. "Hey, Willie. Times two. Jack will be here in a few."

Willie slid the drinks along the bar to Kerri, who drank her own immediately and slid it back for a refill. "Having a rough day, are we, sweetheart?"

Kerri chuckled. She went to Willie's at least twice a week but it wasn't very often that she ordered more than one drink. "Something like that." She decided to down the second one and tapped the bar for Willie to fill it a third time before heading to the back booth to sit.

By the time Jack arrived, she was already sipping on the drink she had ordered for him. "It must be hitting you hard if you are already into your second drink."

Kerri looked down at the empty glass beside her and decided to tell the truth. "More like fourth. Grab us a couple more?"

Jack tilted his head at her and shrugged before dropping his sweater in the booth and making his way to the bar. He waved at Willie from across the room and the drinks were ready by the time he got there. They were the only people in the place at quitting time on a Monday, so service times weren't exactly a problem.

Jack dropped the glasses on the table and flopped himself down across from Kerri in the booth. "I told you that you were still hung up on her. I told you when I said you had to break it off with Savannah. What in the name of god made you think it was a good idea to add her as a friend?"

Kerri gulped. Jack wasn't pulling any punches, but he never did when it came to his opinion on her love life.

"She added me, and I was curious. I couldn't help myself. And then, she sent me a message and I felt bad, I had to respond. I mean, it has been almost seven years. I can't be still hung up on her, you can't be right about that."

"Yes, I can. I don't think anyone really gets over their first love. And there was nothing ever really resolved between you two." Jack huffed. "I know you don't want to hear this either, but I think you should see her."

Kerri bowed her head, watching the liquid move around the glass as she spun it in her hand. "No, no, no. There is no way." She looked Jack directly in the eyes, "That is the worst idea I have ever heard. What good would it do?"

"A lot, if you ask me. You need closure. You need to sit down with her and talk and figure out your feelings.

You need to see that she is happy and then maybe you can find a way to be happy too." They sat in silence for a few moments before Jack reached across the table and gently placed his hand on her wrist.

"You have your interview tomorrow afternoon. Why not suggest meeting up before? It will be a good reason for you to leave if you need. You are never going to move on if you don't let her go." Jack smiled and Kerri returned it weakly.

She kept thinking about the last time he gave her advice. It had been about Savannah. They were dating for four months when they decided to move in together. Jack told her to slow down, she didn't have to fit every stereotype all at once, but she hadn't listened. It was their shared apartment that had given Savannah the impression that Kerri was more serious about the relationship than she actually was. It was the moment that had sent their relationship into the start of its eventual spiral.

"Okay. I'll ask her to get coffee. That's all. And I will set it up for no more than an hour before my interview so that I can excuse myself. I really don't know if this will help anything, Jack." Kerri downed the rest of her drink and slammed the glass a little harder than she expected on the table.

"It will, I promise. Now, let's get you something to eat to soak up all that whiskey and see about sobering you up." Jack grabbed her jacket from the booth and walked her to the door. "Thanks, Willie. You can put it on my tab." He waved as they left.

CHAPTER 10

Kerri had agreed to meet Summer at 11am at The Little Café, the coffee shop just across the street from the North Beach Observer. Kerri bounced in her seat, drummed on the steering wheel, and turned up the music to sing along as she drove. She wasn't sure which made her more nervous, the meeting with Summer or the interview, but she was trying desperately to keep her mind off both as she commuted from Jenkinstown that morning.

She arrived at the coffee shop at 10:52 and decided to order and take a seat to wait. Kerri had no idea what they would say to each other, but just being in the same place as Summer was causing her stomach to flip flop, so she decided to forgo food and only ordered a coffee. She nervously sipped her drink and checked the time as she watched the door for Summer to arrive. Kerri`s eyes lit up and she couldn't help but smile when she finally saw Summer walking toward her. All of her old feelings washed over her in an instant and she wished she had never agreed to meet her.

Summer flipped her hair over her shoulder and didn't even wait until she took her seat to start talking. "You look amazing! Sorry if I'm late, I had to wait for the babysitter. I didn't want to bring Ava, I thought it might be too much for her with all the activity down here. And the traffic! I think the commute downtown gets worse every day. I'm sorry, I'm rambling. You do look great."

Kerri laughed nervously. "Thanks. I have that interview, so I suppose I'm a little more dressed up that usual. You look great too." She blushed. "I would never have known you had a baby." Kerri blurted out before wishing she could pull the words back and swallow them.

Summer smiled shyly. "I'm so glad you decided to meet up. I mean, I never thought you would when I asked. I just, I think about you a lot, wonder if you are okay, and happy. I couldn't believe it when I saw your name in my suggested list of friends. I didn't even think you would agree to that request, never mind this one. Guess I got brave when you replied." She looked over at Kerri and smiled. "I'm rambling again, aren't I?" Kerri nodded. "Sorry. I'm nervous."

"I get it. I'm, ah, I'm nervous too. I never thought I would see you again, after you left." Kerri struggled to find the words.

"I wrote to you. I wrote to you all the time. I sent you dozens of emails, telling you about my life and school but you never replied. Not once." Summer bowed her head.

"I replied. I wrote pages and pages when I received the first few. I just couldn't send it. Then, when I started dating someone, I just stopped reading them. It was too hard for me." Kerri's words stuck in her throat.

"It's alright. I understand. I didn't really expect a reply. I mean, I hoped, but I never expected it after the way that we left things. God, seeing you brings up so much. I think about you all the time." Summer covered her mouth with her hand. "I shouldn't have said that."

Kerri heard the words repeat over and over in her mind. *I think about you all the time*. They sat in silence until

Kerri finally had the nerve to pipe up. "I think about you too. A lot. More than I should. I was hoping that seeing you would make me stop. Jack said that this might give me some closure."

Summer was making intense eye contact through the entire admission, then looked to the floor, blinking back a tear. "I'm sorry I screwed everything up for us."

Kerri's watch started to beep to remind her about her interview. "Oh, shit! Oh god, I'm so sorry. I have to leave. My interview is in ten minutes." She jumped up from the table, almost knocking her remaining coffee over on her lap.

"It's okay. But, um, Kerri?" Summer stood to face her.

"Yeah?"

"I'm not sure what your plan is for after the interview, but I would love to pick this up again. I have the sitter for the whole day and I'm not sure when you will be back in town, but this has been really great. I would love to take you to lunch?"

Kerri struggled to get her arm into the sleeve of her coat and replied without thinking. "That sounds great. I'll meet you back here in an hour?"

"I would really like that." Summer smiled and blushed a little as she helped Kerri adjust her jacket. "I'll see you then." She almost skipped out of the coffee shop behind Kerri.

Kerri rushed across the street to the high rise building that housed the offices of the North Beach Observer. She brushed her hands down the front of the purple dress shirt she had chosen for the occasion and checked to make sure it was properly tucked into her jeans before knocking on the door to the main office.

She was greeted by a young woman, probably about

her age. "You must be Kerri. I'm a big fan of your work."

Kerri extended her hand. "Wow. I didn't think anyone outside of Jenkinstown had ever seen my work. But thank you."

"I'm Julia, one of the junior reporters. Steph is just finishing a phone interview. She will be right with you." Kerri nodded and took a seat against the wall near the office with Editor in big black letters on the door.

She was nervously checking her watch when she heard footsteps and the door swung open to reveal Steph Underwood, editor in chief. To Kerri, she looked a little more like a librarian than an editor with her hair up in a bun and her black-rimmed glasses slipping down her nose just a little. She was much younger than Kerri had expected, only in her thirties and wore a business suit with red sneakers.

Steph noticed Kerri focusing on her footwear. "It's a fast-paced business. No matter how nice you want to look, you have to be ready to run." She extended her hand and Kerri shook it. "Sorry to keep you waiting. I didn't know the mayor would be so long-winded, but you know how it is when you are trying to get the scoop. Nice to finally meet you, Kerri. Why don't you come in?"

Kerri took a seat in the office and fussed with her brief-case, pulling out both the physical portfolio and the CD-ROM she had hastily compiled the day before. "I brought a number of different samples of my work." She reached into her briefcase again. "And here is a hard copy of my CV. I know it isn't much to look at, being that I have had the same job since I graduated, but that is exactly why I would be perfect for this job."

Steph laughed a little. "I should have been clearer on the phone. The interview is just a formality. I am familiar with your work. Three award nominations in five years on the job will get you quite a bit of attention. I was very surprised when you applied for our opening as you were doing so well in Jenkinstown, but I am excited to have you join the team."

Kerri was dumbstruck. She had been prepared to give dozens of reasons why her experience, even though it was in a small town, was the perfect background to help her make the leap to North Beach. "You mean, you're offering me the job?"

"That's right. I wanted you to come in to talk about what your responsibilities would be and when you are able to start. We have company apartments that you can move into as early as next week until you find a place of your own."

Kerri felt a surge of adrenaline run through her and she had to focus to steady her legs from shaking and tapping against the floor. She tried to absorb all of the details that Steph was giving her about her new position, but she was sure she was going to have questions later. "Well, I would have to give a week of notice, at least. So, I could start a week from Monday?"

"That will work just fine. I will have someone in legal draw up the contract and we will fax it out to you in a couple of days. I'll also send you all the details about the apartment, including your rental rate and we will see you in just over a week." Steph smiled.

Kerri stood and reached to shake her hand once again. "Thank you. This is such an amazing opportunity and I can't wait to get started." She quickly packed her things back into her briefcase and headed to the door. "Thank you again."

Kerri left the office in a daze. She sat in her car grinning to herself and trying to calm down a little before making the drive when she remembered she had agreed to meet

Summer for lunch. All she really wanted to do was get home and tell everyone the news but she didn't have a phone number for Summer so she had no way to cancel.

Kerri sighed and got out of the car, making her way across the street to The Little Café where they had met that morning. Summer was standing outside, smiling at her as she approached. "I got us a reservation at one of my favourite lunch places down the block. Do you mind a short walk?"

"Not at all. Sorry I made you wait." Kerri was suddenly glad that she had no way to cancel.

"It's cool. How did the interview go?"

Kerri tried to keep calm as she spoke. "Well, it wasn't really an interview. They asked me to come in to offer me the job."

"Oh my god, Ker, that's amazing! You must be so excited! Tell me everything." Summer grabbed her by the arm and pulled her around into a hug which Kerri quickly pulled away from. "I'm sorry. It just feels so natural to be around you. I shouldn't have done that."

Kerri ran her hands over her sleeves, straightening out her shirt. "It's okay. You just took me by surprise."

As they walked Kerri filled in all the details of her new job and they fell into comfortable chatter about the things going on in their lives. Kerri felt 19 again, like they were making the daily walk home from college together, joking and laughing.

The restaurant Summer picked out was not quite what Kerri had expected. The door was tucked in an alleyway between two buildings. The atmosphere was quiet and even a little romantic with the soft music and the dim lighting. The Maître d' greeted Summer by name when they entered and immediately seated them in one of the booths by the window.

The pair made small talk for a few minutes before falling into the familiarity they always shared, reminiscing about when they first met and catching up on everything that had happened since the last time they had seen each other. They both avoided talking about the reasons it had been so long in the first place.

"You know, I never thought I would say this, but I think I might be able to be friends again. That is, if you want to, of course. I mean, this is nice and I'm going to be moving to the city soon…" Kerri gulped, hoping Summer would interrupt her to reply. "I won't really know anyone here or anything and I know you have your family and you will be going back to work soon and all, but it might be nice, if maybe we could hang out a little or something?"

"Now who is rambling?" Summer laughed. "I think that would be awesome. It has been a long time since I have been this comfortable just sitting and talking with someone. I mean, we came in here for lunch and at this rate we can soon order from the dinner menu."

Kerri glanced at her watch for the first time since they sat down. "Oh, god, you're right! I should get home. I have a resignation letter to prepare and I'm at work on the early shift tomorrow." Kerri stood and pulled a money clip from her front pocket.

"Put that away. I said I wanted to take you to lunch and once it became a celebration, it was really my treat."

"You're sure?"

"Absolutely. You can take me another time. It'll be an excuse to have to see me. I should give you my number." Summer pulled a pen from her purse and jotted the number on a napkin, handing it to Kerri before standing from the table and straightening her skirt. "It has been really nice to see you, Kerri. Nicer than I imagined it would be."

She lifted her arms to offer a hug and Kerri stepped in.

Summer buried her face in Kerri's neck and ran her hands up her back, pulling her closer. They held on to each other as though it was the last time they would ever touch. Kerri pulled back slightly, bringing her hands to rest on Summer's shoulders as they looked deep into each other's eyes.

Summer broke the gaze to glance around the now deserted restaurant before bringing her hand to rest on Kerri's cheek and then wrapping her fingers behind her neck and pulling her in. Kerri bowed her head at the last second.

"I can't do this." Kerri whispered, pressing their foreheads together gently. "You're married, for Christ's sake. And I can't let you break my heart again." Kerri pulled out of the embrace.

"I'm sorry. I shouldn't have done that. You're right. I won't do it again." Summer blushed with embarrassment as her attempt at a bold move was rejected. She quickly made her way to the front counter to pay. They walked together to the place where Kerri parked, glancing at each other from time to time but neither speaking.

Kerri was relieved when they finally arrived at the car. "Well, this is me. Thanks again for lunch. I actually had a really great day with you."

"Me too. I'm sorry if I ruined it," Summer giggled nervously, avoiding eye contact with Kerri. "I don't know what came over me."

"It's okay. Really. I have to get going, but I will call you once I get settled in." Kerri jumped in the driver's seat and adjusted the rearview mirror before backing out of the parking spot. Summer smiled and waved from the sidewalk, watching her drive away.

CHAPTER 11

According to her lease agreement, the company apartment that she would be staying in was fully furnished, so Kerri didn't need to rent a truck. Instead, she decided to store her furniture in her parents' garage until she found her own place. It took most of Saturday afternoon to pack up her belongings and move out of her Jenkinstown apartment, but she was able to jam what she needed to take into her two-door Pontiac Sunfire. It had seemed like a cool choice of car when she bought it the previous year, but she was now learning that a two-door vehicle was not the best thing to have when you are moving your whole life.

Kerri spent Saturday night with her parents after handing her apartment keys to her landlord that afternoon. She felt like a kid again when her mother had insisted that she go to bed before midnight. Eileen didn't want her to be tired when traveling on the highway the next morning. At 26, Kerri finally understood what it was like to set out on her own for the first time. She felt an independence she had not experienced before, and she couldn't wait to start the adventure.

Eileen had cried when Kerri first told her she was moving and was now standing on the front porch crying as they said their goodbyes. "Mom, North Beach is only a three hour drive. You can visit anytime you like, and I'll come home once a month, I promise."

"I know honey. But with Jack moved across the country, and my baby leaving now too, I'm allowed to be at least a little upset." She pulled Kerri in for yet another hug.

"Okay, okay. But you have to let me go. I'm going to be late to meet the landlord with the keys and I'll have to sleep in my car tonight." Kerri hugged her father one more time before jumping in her vehicle and waving as she pulled out of the driveway.

Kerri cranked up the volume on the stereo and belted along with her new Missy Higgins CD as she drove. She kept the album on repeat for the entire ride, trying to learn the words to all of the songs. It was a nice distraction from the anticipation of starting her job the following day and it kept her mind from flashing back to the lunch that she had with Summer the previous week.

Kerri had thought a lot about that moment when they were leaving the restaurant. She thought about what it would have been like to let Summer kiss her, wondered if it would feel the same way it did all those years ago. She had even wished at times that she didn't stop it from happening. But Kerri knew in the back of her mind that it was the right thing to do and if she really did want to try to redevelop their friendship, there couldn't be any confusion that it would be any more than that.

Kerri pulled up to the apartment building right on time and noticed a man standing in the doorway, swinging around a large set of keys like those that a security guard would carry in an old-time prison movie. He saw her approaching and fiddled through the ring of keys to unlock the door. After a quick tour, he handed her the key and left.

It was a beautiful apartment with ten-foot ceilings, hardwood floors, and marble countertops in the kitchen. It was a one bedroom with an ensuite and a full bath off the large carpeted living room where a flat screen television was mounted on the wall. It only took Kerri an hour to haul her bags and boxes out of the car and start to settle in. She was getting more and more nervous about work as she sat alone on the couch and debated calling Summer to get a drink. She was really the only person she knew in the city.

Kerri picked up her cell phone and decided to send a text message to see if Summer was free. Although she really wanted them to be able to be friends, Kerri wasn't ready to meet Summer's husband either. Summer had barely even mentioned his name when they had lunch, and even then, he only came up because she had ignored his phone call. She carefully crafted the words before sending the message.

I'm all moved in! Don't suppose you are free to grab a drink?

Kerri read and re-read the words on the screen as she waited for a reply. She was about to give up and watch Dangerous Minds for the thousandth time when the phone buzzed in her hand.

I can get free. Might have to bring a little person with me though so I'm not sure a bar is a possibility.

Kerri wasn't sure how she felt about Summer bringing Ava. She wasn't a fan of children and she really wanted to have a couple of drinks that night. She was still considering the options when she received a second message.

What if I picked up a bottle of wine and came to check out your new place?

Kerri gulped. Summer had almost kissed her the last time they saw each other and that was in a public place. But Summer had promised that she wouldn't try it again and Kerri really didn't want to be alone.

That sounds like a plan. I'm at 103 Main Street, apartment 24. It's on the third floor.

Kerri started fussing with the décor around the living room and tidying away the last of the boxes that she had planned to leave until the following day when her phone vibrated again.

Cool. See you in ten.

Kerri's heart started to race as she sorted through the boxes to see if she had anything to offer Summer to eat. "At least I stopped worrying about work," she muttered to herself.

It was almost exactly ten minutes later when Kerri heard a knock at the door. She opened it to find Summer alone and holding two bottles of wine. Kerri stood in the doorway, just looking at Summer. "Are you going to invite me in?"

Kerri laughed and stepped back, pulling the door open wider. "Of course, come on in. I thought you said you would have Ava with you?"

"Doug came home early from his poker game, so he has her." She wandered to the kitchen and started pulling open drawers, searching for a corkscrew. "I got a red and a white. I wasn't sure what you liked." She called over her shoulder.

"I'm fine with either. I'm not exactly a connoisseur when it comes to wine, now whiskey on the other hand..."

"Do you have any wine glasses?" Summer was now

opening all the cupboards in her search.

"I thought I saw some in the last cupboard down. The place was furnished so I'm not exactly sure where everything is yet." Kerri fiddled with the coasters on the coffee table and adjusted the couch cushions as Summer entered the room with two glasses of white wine.

"Here you go. I have to say, you look like you need a drink." Summer chuckled, placing her glass on the table. "I'm really glad you called. I wondered if you would."

"I said I was going to, didn't I?"

"Yeah, but after what happened the last time, I wasn't sure you meant it."

They sat sipping the wine and reminiscing about old times for a little more than an hour when Summer offered to get them a refill and came back with a glass each of the red she had brought. "I guess the pinot was pretty good, 'cause we finished that bottle already!"

"Wow, maybe I should slow down. I do have to work in the morning." Kerri placed the glass on the coaster she had neatly set out when Summer arrived. "Should I put on some music or something?"

"You don't have to on my account, and I know how much you hate background noise." Summer smiled, "you know that if you do, we are just going to wind up singing along for the rest of the night."

"That's probably true. We had more than one hairbrush sing along in my bedroom." Kerri replied as she absentmindedly reached out and placed her hand on top of Summer's which Summer had been brushing over the fabric of the couch between them. Kerri wasn't sure why she had done it, but Summer didn't pull away. Instead she softly stroked her thumb over Kerri's little finger in appreciation of the touch.

Kerri inhaled sharply, watching as Summer pulled her hand back slightly, turned it over and softly brushed her fingertips along Kerri's palm. Kerri interlocked their fingers and reached forward to pick up her wine glass from the table, taking a large swallow. They sat silently, both watching their hands as they participated in a thumb war of gentle touches.

Summer squeezed Kerri's hand and turned to face her, moving closer in the process. She was afraid to say anything that would ruin the moment, instead using her other hand to stroke her fingers up and down the soft skin on the inside of Kerri's forearm. Goose bumps formed on Kerri's arm and she could feel the prickle as the hair on the back of her neck stood on end.

"What are you doing?" Kerri's voice was only a whisper, her eyes focused on the motion of Summer's fingers.

"I'm not sure." Summer swallowed hard. "I just needed to touch you. I have needed to be touching you since I saw you the other day. I know I shouldn't be saying this, but I don't know how to keep it in."

"No, you really shouldn't be saying this. Please, don't make this harder for me." Kerri almost choked over the words.

"I can't help it. I haven't stopped thinking about you since you left last week. I spent all of today hoping that I would hear from you, and when I did... I have never been so excited in my life."

"Sum, what are you saying? I mean, this has to be the wine talking." Kerri wanted to stop her feelings, put them in a box and step back, but she couldn't bring herself to pull away from Summer's touch.

"It's got nothing to do with the wine." Summer placed her finger under Kerri's chin and tipped it up to make their eyes meet. She slipped her palm along Kerri's cheek and hungrily pressed her lips to Kerri's, and Kerri returned the passion. Summer pulled back to catch her breath, pressing their foreheads together she whispered, "I'm think I'm still in love with you."

Kerri jumped from the couch. She could feel a slight wobble in her legs, from the bottle of wine she had consumed, as she tried to stand. "It has to be the wine." Kerri pushed her bang back over her head. "I mean, what else could it be?"

"Kerri, breathe. The only thing the wine is doing is making me brave enough to say what's really on my mind." Summer paused. "I regret that I didn't give us a real chance to be together. I regret not listening to you when you tried to assure me. I regret not kissing you the day I told you I was leaving for school. I should have been braver back then. I need to be brave now and I need you to be brave and be honest with me."

"Yeah, but you are *married*. I can't be that person. I can't be someone that you keep on the side and I won't be someone that breaks up a family. You have a husband, and a daughter."

"The end of my marriage would not be on you. It would be because I was finally being true to myself."

Kerri paced the floor in front of the couch, coming to a stop directly in front of Summer. "You want honest?"

"Please. I think we owe each other that."

"I have spent the past seven years trying to get over you. I tried to move on, I tried to be happy. I never really was. I was never not in love with you."

Summer slowly rose to stand face to face with Kerri. She stroked the back of her fingers along Kerri's cheek and tickled her fingertips down the side of her face and neck. "I know. I know." Summer stuttered. "I know this is going to be complicated. I know that I am going to have to make a lot of changes. But right now, I just want to kiss you and know that everything will be okay."

Kerri's body shuddered at the words and Summer's hands on the sides of her neck. "Being here with you like this is all I ever wanted. But it's more than just complicated." Kerri shook her head, she whispered to herself, "If I let this happen, there is no going back."

"There is already no going back." Summer kissed Kerri's cheek. "And I don't want there to be." She brushed her lips along the side of Kerri's face as she spoke, kissing her on the corner of the mouth. "This time, I'm all in." She looked into Kerri's eyes and let her hunger take over, aggressively sliding her tongue along Kerri's lower lip, searching for entry into her mouth.

Kerri's hands began to shake at the action, and she allowed her tentative entry, feeling the softness of Summer's tongue against hers, she leaned her body closer, feeling the heat radiating between them. A cold shiver ran down her back when Summer stroked her hands down over her shoulders leaving them to rest on her hips.

Summer slipped her fingers into Kerri's back pockets and pulled their bodies even closer. Kerri stroked her thumb along Summer's cheek, tilting her head down just enough to part their lips and catch her breath, their foreheads pressed together and noses gently rubbing.

Kerri looked into Summer's eyes, about to speak when Summer's cell phone started to ring in her pocket. Kerri stepped back quickly, averting her eyes as Summer pulled it out. "I have to take this, just one second."

Summer stepped to the other side of the room, flipping open the phone. "Can't you just handle it for a little while longer?" There was a pause as the other party spoke, "Fine. Of course. Sure, whatever. I'll be there in a little while."

Kerri turned her back, trying to seem like she wasn't listening in on the conversation. "Is everything okay?" Kerri bit her lower lip, forcing herself to make eye contact.

"Ava isn't feeling well. She has a cold and is awake for the third time." Summer watched her foot as she scuffed it against the carpet. "Doug is losing his mind. He needs me to come home." She moved across the room quickly to Kerri, grabbing her by the hands. "I'm so sorry. I don't want to leave it like this. Especially with him forcing me out the door. I don't want you to think this is how it is going to be."

"It's okay. I know you have to. We shouldn't have done this, anyway. It was a mistake. Go home to your husband and your baby." A tear was forming in the corner of Kerri's eye and she swiftly wiped her face to keep Summer from noticing.

"You don't mean that." Summer placed her hand on Kerri's neck, stroking her thumb along her cheek.

"It was a mistake. I knew it and I did it anyway." Kerri choked.

"Well, it wasn't a mistake for me." Summer's voice cracked as she spoke.

"Just go home."

Summer kissed Kerri on the temple and tipped her chin up so she could look her in the eyes. "I meant everything I said tonight. Don't doubt that." She turned, grabbed her jacket from the back of the couch and glanced back one final time before closing the door to the apartment.

CHAPTER 12

A tour of the offices and a meet and greet with the staff were the start of Monday morning for Kerri at the North Beach Observer. Her first individual assignment was set for her second day as Steph had insisted she take the first day to get settled in and tag along with one of the other reporters. Kerri was terrible with names and after being introduced to the staff of close to 40 people, she started to wonder if she would know her own name by the end of the day.

She spent the morning break making small talk with Julia, the junior reporter she had met the day she arrived for her interview, and they hit it off immediately. "So, Steph says I should tag along with someone this afternoon. See how you guys operate," Kerri said as she was about to leave the staff room. "I don't really know anyone else, so..."

"That sounds cool. I have a news conference at 1:30, you could come along." Julia replied.

"Awesome. I'll see you then."

Kerri headed back to her desk to try to familiarize herself with the editing software used by the Observer and organizing the assignment list she was given for the week. She barely looked up from the screen and even worked through her lunch hour. The one thing that pulled her focus was her cell phone as it sat beside her on the desk.

Julia found Kerri at 1pm exactly, staring at her phone and debating whether or not she would text Summer. She had not replied when Summer texted her that she was home the night before and was feeling guilty about the fact that she didn't at least acknowledge that she received it. She looked up as Julia cleared her throat to announce her presence.

She was standing above Kerri's desk, already wearing her coat, camera bag slung over one shoulder and a soft briefcase on the other. "Oh, shit! Am I making you late? I'm sorry, I didn't realize the time." Kerri jumped up, sending her desk chair flying into the wall behind her.

"It's okay, we have a couple of minutes." Julia laughed, running her hand over her head to brush her chin-length red hair out of her eyes. "Get your stuff, the press conference starts in 30. Should be a good one. The police are giving an update on a homicide case from last month. I have a theory that it is connected to another killing last year."

Kerri smiled and threw on her coat. "Wow. That will be a first for me. We didn't exactly have a lot of crime in Jenkinstown. Certainly, never had the chance to cover a murder." She grabbed her camera bag and had to practically jog through the office to keep up with Julia.

The car ride was mostly silent, and Kerri's thoughts slipped back to the text message from the night before. *I'm home, we will talk soon?* Kerri wanted to talk now. She had been consumed with thoughts of the taste of Summer's lips that were rudely interrupted by a nauseous feeling in her stomach from the guilt of why she had to leave, or even that they had kissed at all. Kerri had never felt so conflicted.

She was zoned out for most of the drive when Julia started to speak. "Lost in thought, or just taking in the sights?"

Kerri snapped back to reality, flipping her phone over and over in her hands. "Sorry. Just thinking, I guess. It has been a big week."

"I would imagine so. New job, new city, new apartment, new people."

Kerri chuckled under her breath, "Old people."

"What was that?"

"Nothing. You're right. All the new is a little overwhelming." Kerri sighed and looked at her phone again.

"Expecting a call or something? You haven't stopped playing with that thing since we left the office."

"No, I, ah, was... I was just thinking about someone that I should have answered." Kerri slipped the phone back into her pocket.

"It's okay. I didn't mean to pry." Julia pulled the car up in front of the police station and put it in park. "But if you wanna talk, I mean, I'm sure being new in town, you could use a friend. Maybe a drink after work?"

Kerri shifted uneasily in her seat, "Um, yeah. That would be nice, actually."

"Great! Now, let's get in there and see if they know whodunit." Julia slipped her long legs out of the car gracefully, pulling her gear behind her and slamming the door in one swift motion.

Kerri watched Julia as she set up her equipment expertly and laughed with a couple of the other reporters as they arrived. She had made the effort to introduce Kerri to them, and Kerri smiled and nodded but was more interested in watching Julia prepare. She had enough of introductions for one day and figured she would get to know them over time.

They grabbed a pair of seats near the front of the room, Julia whipped out a notepad from her briefcase and Kerri followed suit. She had attended many press conferences over the years, but she suddenly felt like this was her first and she had no idea what to do next. Once everyone was seated, a man in full uniform approached the microphone at the front of the room and Kerri's instincts finally kicked it.

She grabbed her camera and moved from her seat, looking for the best angle to capture the officer. He pulled out his notes and began to speak, but Kerri was only focused on getting the perfect shot. She caught a couple of words from his announcement, including no arrest, person of interest, possible connection and new evidence but she was in the zone and for the first time in more than a week, she hadn't thought about Summer for almost an hour.

When the conference ended she followed Julia to a scrum at the back of the room, trying to pull more information from one of the officers. Kerri moved in behind and snapped a number of pictures before the crowd broke apart. Julia threw her notepad back in her bag and took Kerri by the arm, pulling her out of the room and back to the car.

"We need to get back as soon as possible. This could be a cover story and I don't want to miss the deadline." Julia jumped into the car and slammed it down in gear, pulling on her seatbelt as she turned from the parking lot. "I knew it! I knew they were going to start investigating them like they were connected! The cases are too much alike."

Kerri was flicking back through her photos of the event, already making a mental note as to which would work best if this became front page news. "Hmm? So, they think the same person is responsible for both deaths?"

Julia nodded, "Weren't you listening? Same MO in both cases. Two women, similar description, both last seen at The Closet night club, both with no family in town and both turn up in their own apartments dead a day later. Police don't think they were killed at home, however."

"Wow. That's messed up. Remind me not to go to that club." Kerri laughed.

"It might be right up your alley, not that I should make presumptions about you or anything, I mean, we don't know each other, really." Julia stuttered.

"What is it that you are presuming?"

"Well, it's just that it, it's a gay club." Julia rushed out the words.

Kerri could only laugh. "You were right. I don't announce it when I meet people or anything, but I've been told I give off a vibe. My ex, Savannah, used to call me a hundred-footer."

Julia lifted one eyebrow in confusion. "Because you are..? I don't get it."

Kerri continued to chuckle, "Because you can tell I'm gay from a hundred feet away. Something about the clothes I wear and my 'swagger' she said."

"Well, the Doc Martins were kind of a tip off, but mostly I thought I saw you on a date with a woman at La Bistro when you were in town last week."

Kerri blushed. "It wasn't a date. Just a couple of old friends getting back in touch."

"Well, you could have fooled me. She was certainly acting like you were more than friends. She didn't take her eyes off of you and made every excuse to touch you." Julia quickly back peddled. "Not that I was paying close attention or anything, it's just the reporter curse. Super observant. Question everything."

"Oh, I get it. People watch more than I care to admit. I must have been distracted that day 'cause I never noticed you in the restaurant."

"I was in the back, on a date of my own. I suppose you can imagine that mine was not going as well if I spent most of the meal watching you two." Julia laughed. "I think there is more going on there than meets the eye, at least from her side."

Kerri absentmindedly chewed on the tip of her thumb. "There just might be."

Julia pulled the car into the parking garage below the high rise that housed the Observer offices, undid her seatbelt and sighed heavily before grabbing her bag from the backseat. "Let's get this to print so we can grab that drink we talked about. I want to hear all about this mystery lady."

Kerri grinned and jumped out of the car, brushing her bangs from her face as she picked up her camera bag and double-timed her steps to try to keep up with Julia as they headed to the elevator for the fourth floor. Kerri almost ran off the elevator when it stopped and hustled down the hallway to her office where she threw herself into her computer chair and started work on putting together a photo spread from the event. It was just over an hour later when Julia was once again standing over her.

"Hey, new friend. It's quitting time. I got the story submitted. How goes the photos?"

Kerri closed her editing program and looked up with a smile. "All set. I just emailed them out."

"Wicked. Now, I don't know about you, but I could really use a drink."

Kerri grabbed her leather jacket from the coat hook behind her in her cubical and threw it on as they walked the short hall to the exit. "Make mine a double."

Julia slid along the bench of a booth at the back of Leroy's sports bar, seating them away from the only other people there, a group of older men sitting on stools at the bar watching soccer on the television. Kerri slipped in across from her as a waitress came up beside the pair. Julia quickly ordered a draft beer and Kerri asked for her usual, a double whiskey on ice.

"So, there are a couple of reporters that you should really get to know. Dave is the political guy which means he knows all the scandal that is happening around town and he always has some funny story about what government is up to. He is one of the least annoying guys in the office, knows when to shut up, ya know?" Julia laughed.

"He's the one that was wearing a tie this morning?" Kerri tried to put a face to the name.

"He always is. Says it feels unprofessional to be surrounded by suits and not be wearing one. Steph is pretty cool, too," Julia blushed, "She is harder to get to know than most, tries to keep her distance where she's the boss and all, I think, but she's really down to earth and funny." Julia looked up and flashed a smile and a nod at the waitress who had returned with their drink order.

"That's cool. It's just going to take me a little time to get my footing, you know?"

"Yeah. I hear ya." Julia quickly changed the subject. "So… you feel like talking about the girl from the restaurant? I have to tell you, I'm dying to know if she is the same reason you were constantly checking your phone today."

Kerri's ears turned bright red as her face flushed. "Yep.

Same one. There isn't much to tell really. I mean, she's married." Kerri quickly downed her drink and waved to the waitress for another.

"Shiiit. That makes things complicated. Do you know her wife?"

"Husband."

"Huh? But I thought…"

"And baby." Kerri continued.

"Shiit. But she is obviously feeling more than a friend vibe for you."

Kerri released a breath she didn't realize she had been holding in. She felt at ease with Julia and it was nice to talk to someone about it that didn't know Summer, or her for that matter. She had planned to fill Jack in when they spoke the following night, but she knew exactly what he would say, *be careful. Don't get invested, hell, don't even get involved. Stay away.* She could edit their history with Julia.

Kerri gave her a brief overview of her past with Summer and felt a weight lift from her shoulders when she told Julia about what happened the night before. Julia showed no judgment, even when Kerri ordered a third whiskey before completing the story. Kerri thought Julia was going to fall out of her chair when she mentioned nonchalantly that they had kissed the previous evening.

"And then she had to go, and I told her it was all a big mistake and it never should have happened 'cause it was."

"Well, that really is too bad. You're pretty hung up on her, aren't you?" Julia reached across the table and took Kerri by the hand.

"Why too bad?"

Julia blushed. "Well, you're hot, and single, but you are so off the market."

Kerri's jaw dropped. She didn't think about it when Julia asked her for a drink, but looking back, she could have been asking her out. "Oh god, did I read this wrong? Did you mean for this to be a date? And I'm here spilling my guts about my ex and I don't even know you."

Julia laughed nervously. "I didn't have an expectation. Just wanted to get to know you a little, see what happened. And I'm the one who brought up your ex."

Kerri's phone vibrated on the table. She flipped it open as soon as she saw Summer's name on the screen and found a text message waiting for her.

I really need to talk to you. Is now a good time?

Kerri swallowed hard and looked across the table at Julia. "Ah…"

"It's her, isn't it? It's cool. We can call it a night. I don't know about you, but three is my cutoff for a Monday anyway." Julia smiled sweetly. "Maybe we can get together again? I think we could make great friends."

Kerri nodded. "That would be great. Thanks for the ear tonight… and ah, sorry."

"No need to apologize. I understand."

Kerri's phone vibrated again, another message from Summer.

I want to see you. Are you home? Please Kerri, don't shut me out.

Kerri swallowed the rest of her drink quickly and headed to the bar to pay her tab, replying to the message as she walked.

Be home in ten. I'll meet you there.

CHAPTER 13

Kerri had poured herself a glass of whiskey and was hanging up her coat when Summer knocked. She opened the door to see Summer pleading through puffy eyes and flushed cheeks, swollen from crying. Kerri stepped back from the frame, gesturing to invite Summer into the apartment.

Summer slipped her hands under Kerri's arms and around her back, pressing her face into Kerri's shoulder. Kerri stood for a moment with her arms out to the side before feeling Summer's chest heave and putting them around her. Kerri could smell the sweet aroma of Summer's shampoo mixing with a faint smell of alcohol on her breath as she held her, and Summer squeezed herself tighter into Kerri's chest. Kerri gently rubbed her hands down Summer's shoulder blades then up and grabbed her shoulders and pulled them out of the hug.

"So, are you going to tell me what was so urgent? I mean, it's after ten on a weeknight and here you are messaging to come over." Kerri felt her anger suddenly building, "Your husband can't be too happy that you're out again."

Summer wiped her face with the sleeve of her coat. "I don't care what he thinks. I tried to talk to him, tell him that I'm not happy, and it turned into a huge fight."

"You, you told him that you are unhappy?" Kerri folded her arms across her chest and turned toward the couch. "No, I don't want to know. You talk a big game, but you are really messing with my head. You say all these things, but how do I really know?"

Summer's jaw dropped. She took a couple of steps toward Kerri and rested her hand on her shoulder. "What are you talking about?"

Kerri's lips had loosened from the whiskey and she readied herself to say everything that had been keeping her awake at night. "From the first afternoon we met up. Telling me that you think about me, apologizing for running away from us back in college, taking me to lunch and trying to kiss me! It made me feel the way I used to when I was around you and I wanted to hold on to that."

"Are you saying you don't?"

Kerri cut her off. "Let me finish. It got worse. I spent the next week doing nothing but thinking about that moment, wondering if I made a mistake and if I should have let it happen. That's why I texted you the night I moved in here. I needed to see you to find out how I was really feeling. I needed to know if it was the past coming up, or if I still had feelings for you."

"And?" Summer bit her bottom lip.

"And then you showed up with way too much wine and started saying all of the things that I had been feeling. But you took it one more step, you said you're still in love with me and you made me admit that I have never gotten over you. But here you are again, on my doorstep, mentioning your husband, leaving him to come see me. Getting into a fight with him and then calling me. It's a huge mindfuck, Sum. Huge!"

"I know this is going to sound terrible, but I really need to talk to you about what is going on with him." Summer spoke softly. "You need to understand that I'm not playing games with you. You need to know that I meant all of the things that I have said, even if I blurted most of it out without thinking."

Kerri picked up her whiskey from the table and flopped herself onto the couch with Summer seated at the opposite end. "I'll try to listen. I don't know what difference it is going to make, though."

Summer took a deep breath, "I'll start from the beginning. I met Doug not long after I came here to go to school. I was so completely heartbroken over leaving you and he was nice to me. He made me laugh and we had a lot in common. After a couple of months, we started dating and things went really well. He was sweet and kind and he wanted all of the same things that I did. The biggest problem for me was that I didn't want to have sex with him, so I told him I was waiting for marriage."

Kerri huffed. "Bet that went over well."

"It did, actually. We were dating for a little over a year when he proposed. I guess I had given up on you by that time. I was still sending you emails, but you had never replied, so I sent one final message to ask you to tell me not to marry him, that you would give me another chance. When I didn't hear from you, I said yes."

"I told you, I stopped reading your emails. It was too hard for me to know about your life and not be able to be a part of it."

"I'm not blaming you, Kerri. I just want you to understand how I got here." Summer took a deep breath before continuing. "We put off the wedding until after we finished school, and I spent the entire time looking for a way to push it even more. I didn't want Doug out of my life, but I knew that I shouldn't marry him, that it wasn't fair to him."

"Didn't stop you from eventually doing it anyway," Kerri snarked.

"No, it didn't. I still wanted a family and a home, and he was offering all of those things. I thought I could do whatever it took to make him happy and as soon as I had children I would be too. It was all I ever wanted in life, to be a Mom." Summer paused, trying to find the words to continue.

"You didn't need a man for that, you know." Kerri grabbed the whiskey bottle from beside the couch and re-filled her glass again.

"I suppose I realize that. But there's so much more to the story. The night we got married I convinced myself that it was going to be okay. I put on a good show for the crowd, smiling and being polite to his family. I had barely kissed him in weeks leading up to the day, but he chalked it up to the stress. Then, the time came for us to leave the party behind. We went back to our hotel room,"

"Do I really have to listen to this?" Kerri's stomach rolled just knowing what was about to be said.

"Yes. I need you to hear it. I need you to know that I am not messing with you." Summer kept her eyes focused on the fabric of the couch. "I locked myself in the bathroom when we got to the room. I was pretty drunk, and I knew he was too, so I figured if I stayed in there long enough, he would pass out. I didn't wait long enough. He was still awake and drinking champagne when I emerged in my flannel PJs. He, he wouldn't take waiting another night for an answer, so we did it." Tears formed in Summer's eyes.

"Are you saying he forced you?"

"No, I didn't say no, I didn't try to stop him. I just cried the entire time and let my mind wander to anywhere else." She looked up at Kerri, "Mostly I thought about you."

"Here we go again with the mindfuck." Kerri stood from the couch, unsteady on her feet from the whiskey.

"It was the only time I let it happen. He got angry and distant when I turned him down or found a way to keep him from trying after that. Three weeks later I found out I was pregnant with Ava. Doug was ecstatic and stopped pressuring me, instead spending more and more nights out of the house with his friends, going to clubs. He said it was his last hurrah before we had a baby and his life had to change."

Kerri gripped the arm of the sofa to sit down again. "I still don't know why I have to hear all of this. What are you hoping to accomplish?" she slurred.

"Please, just listen. This is the part that might even be harder for you to accept. I was about six months pregnant when after work on a Friday, Doug had won a big case that day, and he wanted us to go to dinner and celebrate. It was a tradition we had since we first started working in the public defender's office. We went to a Chinese place near the office and I happened to know one of the women waiting for a table. We chatted casually for a few minutes while Doug spoke to the waitress." Summer swallowed hard.

"So, what's the big deal?" Kerri was getting more and more snarky.

"Well, when he came to get me, he asked who she was. I didn't speak and she told him that we had a "little thing" once. Doug grabbed me by the arm and dragged me out of the restaurant. He screamed at me on the sidewalk, demanding to know what she had meant. It was a one-night stand and it was years ago, before Doug proposed. He couldn't handle it. He said some pretty nasty things about how I told him I wanted to wait and what that did to him before screaming the word dyke and telling me to find my own way home."

"Wow. That's intense." Kerri pulled her knees to her chest.

"Yeah. Intense. He didn't come home for three days. He wouldn't answer my calls and he didn't show up for work on Monday. I thought about reporting him missing, but the truth was... I hoped that he never came back. He showed up at home Monday evening, acting like nothing ever happened and he has never brought it up again until tonight. He got more distant after that though, angrier about anything and everything."

"I can't believe you let him stay." Kerri poured herself another glass of whiskey despite her better judgment. The alcohol was making the conversation hurt less, but she would be hurting for work in the morning. "I also can't believe you slept with another woman." She slurred.

"It's not like you haven't." Summer snapped back.

"Woah, no need to get defensive. I just didn't know is all. I'm not sure how I would, but that's not the point."

"What is the point?" Summer spoke more controlled.

"I don't know... I still don't understand what you are doing here."

Summer moved closer to Kerri on the couch. "He got really angry, asking about people I was talking to on Facebook and where I was the other night. After he screamed that word at me again, the only answer I could muster was, so what if I am? He grabbed me by the arm and I really thought he was going to hit me, but he didn't. He just grabbed his jacket and left. Ava is with his mother and I didn't want to be alone. I think he knows there is someone else, but he doesn't know that it is you."

"Don't you have other friends? Why would you come to me?" Kerri's head was starting to spin from the whiskey.

"Because I'm not messing with you, Ker. I didn't want to be around anyone else. I had to see you. You were the best friend I ever had and the only person that I wanted to see tonight. I meant what I said. I am still in love with you."

Kerri struggled to keep her eyes open. She could barely take in the words that Summer was saying through the fog of alcohol and sleep. "I have to go to bed. I think you should go. Please, can we talk more tomorrow?"

"You should go to bed and I know this is a lot to ask, but can I stay? I don't want to go home alone, and I really don't want to be there if he comes back. I'm not asking you for anything other than a place to sleep."

"I can't have you that close to me..." Kerri's voice trailed off at the admission as she glanced between Summer and the hallway to the bedroom.

Summer reached out and took Kerri by the hands. "I'm not asking you for anything like that. I want to be near you, to be with you, but not like this. Not tonight. Especially not when you are this drunk."

"I'm fine. I just can't deal with falling asleep next to you or waking up with you in my bed. I understand that you can't go home, but I can't do this either."

"How about I just stay right here, on the couch. Would you be okay with that?"

Kerri looked around the apartment, grabbing her com-

126 The Love of Summer

fy blanket from the back of a chair before getting a pillow out of the linen closet in the hall and a beer t-shirt from her drawer. She handed the items to Summer. "On the couch. Okay." She staggered off to the kitchen, downing a full glass of water and pouring a second to take to bed.

Summer was already under the blanket, her jeans and hoodie folded neatly on the coffee table when Kerri returned to the room. "Thanks for this Ker. I'm so glad you let me come over tonight."

Kerri just nodded as she headed down the hall to her room. "Sleep well. I'll see you in the morning."

CHAPTER 14

Kerri got out of the shower and glanced out into the living room to find Summer was still sound asleep on the couch the next morning. Her head was foggy from the half a bottle of whiskey she had consumed the night before and the last thing she wanted to do was go to work. She dressed quickly, and as quietly as possible, to keep from waking the sleeping woman and was all but out the door when Summer finally stirred on the couch.

"Headed out? What time is it?" Summer said groggily.

"Just after seven. Sorry if I woke you. There are fresh towels in the bathroom if you wanna grab a shower here."

"Thanks. I really appreciate you letting me stay." Summer stood from the couch, keeping the blanket wrapped around her waist.

"It's fine. I'm going to be late. Just lock the door on your way out, okay?" Kerri closed the door behind her and took a deep breath before making her way down the hall of the apartment complex and racing down over the three flights of stairs to the street.

Kerri grabbed a protein shake instead of her regular black coffee at The Little Café before heading into the office. She tried her best to keep smiling as she opened the door and was immediately greeted by Julia. Kerri rushed past her to her cubical, trying to avoid questions about the text message that had made her ditch Julia at the bar the previous evening.

Kerri hung up her coat and turned back to her desk, startled as Julia appeared in the doorway of her cubicle. Julia held her hands in the air in surrender. "I'm not here to pry. There was another homicide last night. This time the body was found just behind The Closet. Police think security scared the killer away before he had a chance to move her body."

"That's crazy. Do they have any leads?"

"I guess we will find out soon enough. There's another press conference this morning and you are now officially on this story with me, so grab your stuff."

Kerri did as she was told and followed Julia out of the building. She was glad there was going to be some action happening to distract her from the night before, and also glad that Julia was more interested in the news story than what had happed after Kerri arrived at home the previous night. They drove in silence to the police station, listening to the latest radio report on what was happening at the scene.

The room at the police station was filled with reporters and official looking people when Kerri and Julia entered. The police chief took to the podium just as Kerri was setting her camera and began by clearing his throat to get the attention of the audience. Kerri took a couple of quick shots and moved to the other side of the room to focus her attention on several posters that showed an artist description of the suspect.

The police chief motioned for the reporters to lower

their hands and proceeded to make his statement. "Please leave all questions until the end. So, at approximately 23:42 last evening police were called to the alley behind the nightclub known as The Closet. When they arrived on the scene, officers found the body of a 22-year-old woman that we have not yet identified. She was severely beaten, and we believe the incident is connected to two other deaths that have occurred over the past four months."

There were several camera flashes as the chief picked up the artist rendering and continued. "In the incident last night security at the club were alerted to an argument happening in the alley. One security guard entered the area to find a man straddling over the woman and repeatedly hitting her. He called 9-1-1 after chasing the man from the area but was unable to revive the woman. He was, however, able to give us a description of the suspect."

The chief shuffled the papers on the podium in front of him. "The suspect in the case has been described as Caucasian, approximately six foot in height, 220 pounds with sandy blonde hair. He was wearing a black button-down shirt under a grey windbreaker style jacket and dark blue jeans. He is considered potentially armed and dangerous. If you see a man matching this description, you are asked to avoid confrontation and contact police immediately. We have several copies of the sketch available at the front and it has been sent via email to every major media outlet in the city. Questions?"

A voice from the back of the room perked up, "Does this mean that police believe all of the women were killed in the alley and then taken from the scene?"

The chief wiped his fingers down over his moustache and the corners of his mouth. "We do now have reason to believe that the alley was the scene of the initial crimes, we cannot be sure, however, that they were killed in the alley. We believe our suspect may have been spooked and finished the job earlier than he would have liked."

Julia was next to raise her hand. "Will police be increasing their presence around the club and the neighbourhood where these incidents have occurred?"

"We have already increased the number of patrols in that area and will be watching the club and the alley closely after 2200 hours, seven nights a week."

Another voice from across the room jumped in next. "The rest of the murders took place on a weekend. Do police have any reason to believe that this is not connected because many of the details are different?"

"Not at this time. As I stated, we believe the suspect was sloppy in this case. He may have heard the security team and was forced to change his plans."

"One further question?" Julia piped up, "are police looking at these killings as hate crimes? He is targeting gay women, correct?"

"We have not made that determination yet, but we do believe the attacks are very targeted to that demographic. Thank you. That is all for now." The chief stepped away from the podium and quickly through a door at the back of the room.

Kerri packed away her camera and chased Julia out the door to her car. "Those were some good questions you managed to get in back there."

"Thanks. I watch too many cop shows, I suppose, but I also live in that neighbourhood, so I'm invested in what the police are doing to stop these killings." Julia sighed.

Kerri just nodded in agreement and pulled her cell phone from her pocket. She had received a text message during the press conference but hadn't bothered to check it as she was torn about whether she wanted to hear from Summer or not. Kerri flipped open the phone to find a message from Jack.

Just saw the news. Call me later?

Kerri quickly replied.

Working, sorry. Just got this. Call you after dinner my time?

She was about to pocket the phone again when the familiar buzz started in her hand.

Perfect. Talk then.

Kerri slipped the phone back in her pocket and glanced at Julia who was giving her a sly smile from the driver's seat. "My brother. He just heard about the murders."

Julia laughed, "well, that's no fun. I figured after you ran off last night you might have a certain someone checking in on you today."

"That is a much longer story that I don't think I should get into now. We have enough going on and only a couple of hours until the deadline. You get writing the story, I'm going to take a walk to the scene, see if I can get a few candid shots of the officers if they are still mingling in the area."

"Great idea. I know the night crew got a few when they first found out, but it would be nice to get a few shots in the daylight." Julia slammed the car door and headed into the building. "See you in a bit."

The wind had picked up and whipped between the buildings as Kerri walked to The Closet. She kept her head low to avoid the sand blowing off the sidewalk getting in her eyes. She now wished she had driven to the scene, but with a large number of one-way streets in the downtown and not a lot of experience driving in North Beach, she felt more comfortable walking.

The wind died down as she turned the corner onto a new block and Kerri looked up to find Summer about a hundred meters away, standing on the sidewalk with a man. Kerri could faintly hear their conversation.

"I'm glad you agreed to meet me. We should talk about what happened last night." Doug rubbed his hand along the back of his neck.

"We should talk about what is going to happen from here. The house is mine, so I expect you to pack your bags and be out by the end of the week."

"Come on, Sum. This is ridiculous. Is this about that woman, the one from the restaurant again? I said I was sorry for calling you that word. You just know how I feel about it, about those people. I know you aren't one of them, you were just confused." Doug grabbed her by the arm.

"I'm not confused, in fact things are clearer than they have ever been. You're just a bigot. I don't want to fight about this anymore in the street." Summer tried to pull her arm free.

"If you don't give me another chance, I'm going to make your life a living hell. I'll fight you for custody of Ava. Don't think I won't. Just say you'll give me one more chance to make this work."

Kerri had almost reached them when she noticed the possessive way the man was holding Summer by the arm. She bowed her head, hoping to breeze past them without drawing attention to herself. She saw fear in Summer's eyes and decided to wave as she passed.

"Hey Kerri! Fancy meeting you here."

Kerri swallowed hard. "Hey yourself." She scuffed the toe of her shoe along the sidewalk and Summer grinned.

Doug let go of Summer's arm to watch the interaction.

"You plannin' on introducing me?" He drawled.

"Sorry, Doug this is Kerri she's my... was my neighbour the year I lived in Jenkinstown. Kerri, this is my husband, Doug."

Kerri gritted her teeth and extended her hand to shake with Doug. His palms were sweatier than she had expected but she held her grip firm trying to show confidence. "Nice to meet you, Doug." Kerri attempted a smile.

"Haven't you all been spending quite a bit of time together lately?" Doug sneered and stared at Kerri. "Is she who you were out with last night?"

Kerri and Summer exchanged glances before Summer spoke up. "We did get together the other week for a nice lunch when Kerri was in town."

"Well, I'm glad you had a nice time together. It was nice to meet you, Kerri, but we really should be going." Doug took hold of Summer's arm and they started back down the street.

Kerri turned to watch them go, as Summer looked back at her, mouthing the words *I'm sorry*. Kerri's mind was racing, wondering if Doug knew more about their meetings. The introduction had given Kerri a lot more insight as to why Summer struggled with his imposing and manipulative behavior.

There were still a number of cops intermixed with people who worked at the club hanging around the scene when Kerri arrived at The Closet. She kept her distance, so she was able to quickly capture the uninterrupted expressions of the group as they milled around, waiting for news. Within ten minutes she thought she had the perfect shot and hustled back to the Observer to get it submitted.

At the end of the day Kerri couldn't wait to crash on her couch with a little whiskey and throw on the Amy

Winehouse album she had just bought. Her song "Rehab" had been all over the radio since Kerri saw her perform it on the MTV Movie Awards the previous week, so Kerri purchased the album for herself as a late birthday gift. She was only a couple of songs into the album when her phone buzzed in her pocket.

Forget about me, sis?

"Jack, shit." Kerri dumped a couple of shots of whiskey over fresh ice and turned down the stereo to make the call.

Jack picked up on the first ring. "Hey there little sis. You keeping out of trouble?"

Kerri laughed. "As much as I always am, I suppose. Getting settled in here at the apartment and work is going well. Been hanging out a little with Summer" She breezed over the statement. "How are Martha and the kids?"

"They are doing fine. Adjusting well to the move... but just back that up for a second. Hanging out with Summer?"

Kerri giggled nervously before rolling into the whole story of the time they had been spending together. She glossed over or left out entirely anything that was not a PG conversation between them, instead she focused more on how guilty she was feeling after meeting Doug in the street that afternoon.

"So, I probably don't need to worry about you hanging out at the club that has been all over the news if you are working the married woman angle, not that I'm judging." Jack chuckled. "Just don't get too attached, okay Ker? You know how these things go. They say they are going to leave, but they never do, and you just wind up someone's dirty little secret. You are better than that Ker and you deserve more."

"How do you do that? It's like you reach into the back of my brain and pull out all of the things that I am afraid of and say them out loud so I have to deal with them." Kerri sighed. "I know its cliché, but I think it could be different this time if she was single and I really do think she is going to leave him."

"No matter what happens, I'm your brother and I'll support you. I will be here for you, no matter what. Murder someone? I'm bringing the shovels. But if she hurts you again, don't think I won't be saying I told you so."

Kerri could hear a baby crying in the background and knew that her time to talk to her brother was getting short. "I know you will. And I promise, I won't be going anywhere near that club. I don't need the distraction right now, I have enough to deal with in figuring out this whole thing with Summer."

"Alright. Just be safe. And take care of yourself. I have to go, looks like nap time ended a little sooner than I thought it would. Call again soon?"

"For sure. Same time next week maybe?"

"Sounds good. Love you little sis."

"Love you too, Jack." Kerri closed the phone and walked to the stereo to start the CD from the beginning.

CHAPTER 15

The police weren't offering any new details on what had now been dubbed The Closet Murders when Kerri arrived at the office on Wednesday morning. The first couple of days on the job had been a wild ride, so Kerri was glad for a quiet morning. It would give her a chance to work on a couple of fluff pieces she had been assigned as filler for the weekend edition of the paper.

Kerri left several messages for people that she was asked to feature in the local business segment and spent most of the morning playing around with the layout and editing software she still hadn't become accustomed to using. It was midafternoon when she finally looked up from the screen and realized that she had skipped lunch. She had been so engrossed in her work that she didn't even notice the three text messages and a missed call on her cell phone, all from Summer.

Sorry if yesterday was weird. Can we get together later?

Ava is with her grandma tonight and Doug has poker with the boys from the office. A drink?

The missed call was next. Kerri wanted to be able to put the phone down, but she couldn't help feeling a little giddy that Summer wanted to see her again so soon. She felt a little guilty when she read the final message Summer had sent.

Fine. If you don't want to see me, I get it, but could you at least reply?

Kerri shook her head and took a deep breath, considering what she was going to say.

Hey, sorry. I wasn't ignoring you. Busy at work. I would really like to get a drink. But let's go out somewhere. How is La Bistro at 8?

Kerri was about to put the phone away when it buzzed again.

Perfect. I'll be there.

Kerri almost skipped to the elevator and down the street to her apartment at the end of the day. It had been a long time since she was this excited to see someone and the excitement was even keeping her guilt at bay. She rushed around her place, tidying up from the night before and the rampage in which she had left the house that morning.

She ripped off her work outfit and threw on her favourite jeans with a black fitted tank top and the plaid, long sleeve, button up shirt she had stolen from her brother's closet the night she helped him pack to move in with Martha five years ago. She thought of it as her lucky shirt after she wore it on her first date with Savannah and she was hoping it would have the same effect tonight.

Kerri carefully laced her Doc Martins and placed a slight roll in the cuff of her jeans before grabbing her keys and heading to the restaurant. She walked through the door at 7:55 to find that Summer had not yet arrived, so she found a place at the bar and ordered her usual.

"Drinking alone?" Julia ran her hand along Kerri's lower back as she entered the restaurant and crossed behind Kerri's bar stool.

"Fancy meeting you here. I'm just waiting for someone." Kerri couldn't help but smile.

"Must be the lady you are so hung up on, based on that grin? Mind if I join you while you wait?" Julia gestured to the empty bar stool on Kerri's left.

"I, ah… Sure. I mean, she seems to be running behind anyway." Kerri checked her phone for the third time since she sat down as the bartender placed her glass in front of her.

"I'll take a Corona. I could use a drink after yet another horrible date." Julia chuckled. "I have to stop meeting people on eHarmony."

Kerri tilted her head, "Why would you need to meet people online?"

Julia placed her hand on Kerri's forearm, "well, it seems that I am a little shy and when I do get the guts to talk to someone or ask them out, they are always taken." Julia shrugged and took a swig from her bottle. "At least this way I know the person is single when I send them a message."

Summer was standing in the doorway of the restaurant and watching the exchange between Kerri and a redheaded woman. Her stomach rolled when she watched the red head stroke Kerri's arm and flash a flirtatious smile. She marched up to the bar to make her presence known. "I hope you haven't been waiting long." She flipped her hair over her shoulders and placed her hand on Kerri's back. The redhead turned to face the liquor bottles at the back of the bar.

"No, just a couple of minutes. Fortunately, I have pretty good company."

Summer huffed and pushed herself up on the bar stool to Kerri's right. "That's good, I guess. I don't think we have met?" Summer extended her hand in front of Kerri toward the redhead.

"Oh, sorry. Summer, this is Julia, one of the reporters that I work with. We have been working The Closet Murders together all week. Julia, this is… Summer." Kerri wasn't sure how she should describe their relationship, especially to Julia who seemed to be able to read her like a book.

"Oh, so this is the one that has had you chained to your phone all week!" Julia took Summer's hand. "Pleased to finally put a name and a face to the mystery girl."

Summer scoffed and lowered her eyebrows, "And what brings you to be having drinks with Kerri this evening?"

"So, it turns out, people can pretty much say whatever they like on their dating profile. Third time this week I have met up with someone that I spoke to online and they turned out to be either ten years older than they said, nothing like the profile picture they put up, or in the case of tonight, barely legal."

"So, you use those dating sites a lot, then?" Kerri inquired.

Julia chuckled and placed her hand on Kerri's shoulder, "More lately. I haven't really been comfortable with the club scene since the first murder in December and other than going to work, I don't get much chance to meet people. But you get it, Ker."

Kerri nodded, being a reporter often meant long hours, late nights and early mornings.

Summer cringed at the sound of Julia calling Kerri by a nickname and grew more and more uncomfortable with her level of flirting. She dropped her hand below the bar and placed it on Kerri's knee, softly running her fingernails along the edge of her thigh. "I was hoping to get you alone." She leaned in to whisper in Kerri's ear, letting her lips linger a little too close for a little too long.

Kerri shivered and her eyes pleaded with Julia to make an excuse and walk away, but Julia seemed to have no intentions of leaving any time soon. Kerri could tell she was flirting and that it was making Summer jealous, but she also enjoyed the attention and having two women competing over getting hers.

The banter continued between the three for close to an hour with Summer pressing the boundaries of trying to turn Kerri on and Julia giggling at all the right moments and offering small touches to show her interest. Kerri stood to order another round of drinks, slipping off the edge of the bar stool slightly and catching herself in Julia's lap by grabbing onto her thighs.

"I'm so sorry. I'll just get us those drinks now."

Julia brushed Kerri's bang out of her eyes and smiled up at her. "No need to apologize. But I think you do owe me a drink after that."

Summer jumped off her stool staring at the pair. Kerri glanced back as Summer grabbed her coat and headed out the door and into the street. Kerri's eyes widened as she watched her go. Without thinking she grabbed her own jacket, threw a 20 on the bar and ran after Summer. She didn't even pause to offer a goodbye or an apology to Julia, who was now left alone at the bar.

"Summer! Come on, Summer, wait up!" Kerri yelled after her, chasing her down the street. "Sum!" She screamed and Summer finally came to a stop and turned in her direction. Kerri picked up her pace to a jog to close the distance between them. "What just happened?"

"What? What do you want Kerri? You agreed to meet

me tonight, I showed up to find you flirting with another woman at the bar. You proceeded to practically ignore me and continue to flirt with her for the last hour and now you are acting like you are surprised that I left!" Summer's voice was getting louder and louder and a couple of people on the street had now turned to watch.

"Can we not do this here? We don't need the whole neighbourhood listening to us argue about this." Kerri whispered through gritted teeth. "I wasn't ignoring you. I'm sorry. Can we just go somewhere and talk about this like grownups?"

Summer sighed and let her shoulders relax a little of the jealous tension they had been holding. "Yeah. We can do that."

Kerri took Summer by the wrist and led her down the street and over to her apartment building. Without saying a word, they climbed the stairs to the third floor and Kerri slipped the key into the lock on her door.

The door was barely closed behind them when Summer started. "I can't believe you would flirt with her like that with me sitting right next to you!" She gave Kerri the once over as she removed her jacket. "You look great, by the way."

"Thanks." Kerri bowed her head. "I didn't mean to flirt with her. I was just enjoying the attention. It's not like that kind of thing happens to me every day. Besides, I'm not actually interested in Julia. We work together."

"So, that is the only reason? You work together?" Summer's jealously bubbled up again.

"No, that's not the only reason!" Kerri took a deep breath, trying to control the volume of her voice and keep the conversation calm. "I really want to see what is happening with us. But then I saw you with Doug yesterday and I felt so guilty about everything that's happened."

"You shouldn't be the one that feels guilty. That's all on me." Summer flopped onto the couch and Kerri sat beside her, their knees pressed together. "I am going to leave him. Not for you, but for me. But also, because I want to be with you. He's just making it a little harder than I thought it would be, like threatening to fight me for custody." Summer looked into her eyes and placed her palm on Kerri's cheek.

Kerri's breath caught in her throat. Her eyes were glossed with tears that wouldn't fall as she allowed herself to hope that they could find a way to make things work. She allowed herself to hope that Summer was telling the truth, that she really would leave, and they could finally be together, the way Kerri believed they always should have been.

With one sweeping movement Summer ran her hand behind Kerri's neck and leaned in, forced Kerri's shoulders to the arm of the couch and hungrily pressed her lips to Kerri's, running her tongue along her lower lip, begging for entry. She pulled away slightly, pressing her lips along Kerri's jaw line, down her neck and across her collar bone.

Kerri moaned slightly, her hands wanting to take things further, but her mind knowing that she had to let Summer set the pace. Summer ran her hands down Kerri's sides and slowly undid her belt before slipping her fingers under Kerri's tank top and running her hands back up to her chest, taking the shirt with them. She stopped when she reached her breasts, gently caressing until she could feel the hardening of nipples through the fabric of Kerri's sports bra.

Kerri could no longer hold back, scratching her nails

up Summer's back and expertly unhooked the clasp of her bra. Summer released her lips from Kerri's neck and pulled her shirt up over her head before pulling Kerri forward enough that she could also remove her tank top and bra. Kerri pulled Summer's body down onto her own, feeling the heat of her flesh against her own skin.

"Your skin is so soft; I love the way you feel against me." Kerri looked into Summer's eyes for a reaction.

Summer balanced her weight and reached down, quickly popping open the button on Kerri's jeans and wrapped her leg over Kerri, pinning her to the couch. Summer pulled herself onto her knees and flipped her hair over her shoulder. She bit her lower lip between her teeth as she slowly pulled down Kerri's zipper.

Kerri's eagerness grew as she watched the bounce of Summer's breasts when she moved. Kerri grabbed her by the waist of her pants and pulled her back down into an aggressive kiss. She felt Summer's nipples harden as they pressed against her own and scratched her nails leaving red lines down Summer's back and causing her to whimper and rock her hips against Kerri.

Kerri grabbed Summer's shoulder blades and kissed from her collar bone down, taking one of her erect nipples into her mouth and gently sucking. Summer moaned louder, stroking Kerri's breast and flicking her nipple between her fingertips. Kerri's body answered with a thrust of her hips and a river of gratitude pooling in her underwear.

Kerri kissed across Summer's chest, softly running her tongue in circles around her other nipple. She grabbed Summer by the hips, feeling the roll of her body against Kerri's thigh. Kerri pressed her lips up Summer's chest and along her neck until they were face to face. Summer gently nipped her teeth against Kerri's lower lip and ran her tongue across the tip of Kerri's before Kerri pulled her into a harder, more passionate embrace.

Kerri broke the kiss and pressed their foreheads together to catch her breath. "You're sure you want to do this?"

Summer looked deep into Kerri's eyes and smiled coyly. "Positive." She ran her palm over Kerri's cheek and her thumb across her lips. "Bedroom?"

Summer shifted her weight to pull her body from the couch and took Kerri by the hand to pull her to her feet. She slid her hands down Kerri back and down into her underwear, squeezing her ass just a little before moving her hands to Kerri's sides and pushing the clothing to the floor. Kerri flexed at the knee, pushing her underwear down further before stepping out of her clothing and pulling Summer along by her waistband to the room.

Kerri closed the door behind them, pressing Summer's wrist to the door above her head with one hand and using the other to finish removing Summer's clothes. Summer wrapped her free arm around Kerri's back and stepped forward, taking control again, throwing Kerri to the bed and crawling on above her, kissing her hard.

Kerri tickled her fingers along Summer's inner thigh, feeling her wetness as it trickled down her leg. Kerri could no longer hold back, slipping her fingers along Summer's folds before gently pressing them inside her. Summer moaned with every touch and rocked her body into the penetration, groaning and digging her nails into Kerri's biceps.

"God you are amazing," Summer whispered.

"You ain't seen nothing yet." Kerri said coyly, "I love that you are so wet."

Kerri watched the sweat glistening on Summer's chest as she moved onto her knees to deepen the rocking motion. Kerri felt a tightening within Summer and watched her body shudder above her with the release before she collapsed on top of Kerri, gently brushing her lips against Kerri's neck.

Kerri could feel Summer's wetness dripping down into her own and a pulsing between her legs, warning her of how close she was to a release. She smoothed the tips of her fingers across Summer's shoulders, feeling the press of her chest as she struggled to catch her breath.

Summer swallowed and shifted so half her body was now against the bed. She ran her fingers across Kerri's chest and down her stomach, tracing lines from one crease of her thigh to another. Kerri's breathing shuddered with every caress, "God, please, I'm dying to feel your hands on me, I need you to know how wet you make me." Kerri begged.

Summer smiled up at Kerri and kissed her softly as she finally moved her hand down and gently stroked between Kerri's legs. The initial touch was almost enough for Kerri who had to focus on her breathing to make it last more than a moment. Summer took Kerri's nipple into her mouth as she stroked and groaned as Kerri's body thrashed and her muscles contracted beneath her, finally feeling the release.

"Oh god, you have to stop," were the only words that Kerri could muster. Summer removed her hand and kissed Kerri softly before she placed her head on Kerri's chest and pressed her body to Kerri's side.

Kerri stroked Summer's hair and Summer brushed her fingers along Kerri's arm as they remained, limbs intertwined, both breathing hard. Summer shifted as though she was going to leave, but Kerri pulled her closer. "Please stay. Just stay like this for a few minutes at least?"

"Only a few. I wish I could stay longer, but I really should get home."

The knot threatened to return to Kerri's stomach, but she pushed it down, closed her eyes and focused only on the moment they had shared. Kerri closed her eyes, taking in the scent of Summer, never wanting to be without her again.

CHAPTER 16

Kerri did not remember Summer leaving the apartment when she woke to the sound of her alarm the next morning. Kerri stretched her arm across the bed in search of her body but found only a pillow with a folded piece of note paper taped to it. Kerri rubbed her eyes and grabbed a T-shirt from her nightstand before wrapping the sheet closer around her and pulling the note from the pillowcase.

Kerri,

I'm sorry that you are waking up without me. I'm sorry that I couldn't stay, even though I wanted nothing more in this world than to remain wrapped in your arms. I need you to know that I didn't leave because of him. I left for my daughter, so I could be there when she woke up.

I stayed for as long as I could, watching you smile in your sleep, feeling the warmth of your skin against mine and yearning to remain beside you. I have never felt more safe, secure or loved than I did in that single moment of passion with you last night. I can still feel the touch of your hands and the softness of your lips against mine as I sit beside you and write this.

You are incredible. Tonight has been incredible. Thank you for reassuring me with every step and making me feel the way I truly believe only you can. I know things are complicated, but it won't be this way forever. Please hang in there and take this journey with me.

I should have said this last night, reminded you that I love you and I want only you. I won't be able to get away tonight, but I can't wait until the next moment that I can hold you in my arms and be held by you. I am counting the minutes until I can see you again.

Love always,

Sum

Kerri was racked with guilt as she read the words over and over again. It wasn't just that Summer was married, there was also a child involved and she wasn't just getting in the middle of a relationship, she was part of breaking up a family. Kerri knew all the things Summer said about being unhappy with Doug and that she was not the reason for leaving, but a piece of her could not let go of the idea that it was all her fault.

Kerri picked up her cell phone to check for messages but had to put it away to convince herself not to message Summer. She read the note again before putting it in her nightstand and jumping in the shower to get ready for the day.

It was a slow day in news, so most of Kerri's morning was spent researching and editing a few pieces she was keeping in reserve to lighten her summer workload. She had joined Julia for an awkward meal in the lunchroom. She pressed for details about what had happened when Kerri left the bar the previous evening.

"There really isn't much to tell." Kerri lied, pushing the food around on her plate.

"You are almost glowing this morning. I never figured you for the don't kiss and tell kind of girl. Come on, give me a little something?" Julia prodded.

"I don't know what you want to hear. I chased her down in the street, no thanks to you by the way…" Kerri darted her eyes at Julia.

"Yeah, I should apologize for that. People tell me I am a big flirt. I was just getting a kick out of the reaction I was getting, from the both of you, I should add." Julia laughed, "She was so jealous! I really didn't mean to take it that far, though. I can only guess it didn't do too much damage to the rest of your night?"

Kerri sighed, "I'm not mad about it. I think it all worked out for the best, in the end. But I'm sure as hell not getting into details with you. Suffice it to say we had a good talk and a really nice night."

"You're totally blushing! Say no more. I know exactly what kind of nice night you had."

The knot in Kerri's stomach was getting bigger the more she thought about the ecstasy she had felt being with Summer the night before. She checked her phone when she returned to her cubical to find a text from Summer that made it worse.

Don't message me for a while. Doug is on a rampage about how late I came home. I'll be in touch. I love you.

Kerri knew that Doug had to be suspicious about where Summer had been and who she had been with until well after midnight. Kerri struggled to focus on her work so, instead, she packed up her camera bag and knocked on the office door down the hall that read "Editor-in-Chief." Steph Underwood threw open the door, appearing once again in her business suit and sneakers.

"Kerri! What can I do for you? I know we haven't had a chance to chat since you started, but it's great that you and Julia have been working so well together." She stepped back from the entranceway and gestured for Kerri to enter, closing the door behind them. "Take a seat. Tell me, how has the first week been treating you?"

Kerri fussed to pull the strap of her camera bag over her head and sat in the same chair where she had first met Steph just a couple of short weeks ago. "Things are going great from my perspective as well. Julia is a great reporter and has been wonderful about showing me around the city and helping me get adjusted to all the new programs and procedures."

"Wonderful. I knew you would make a good team. And how are you adjusting to city life?"

"It's good. Julia has been helping with that as well, taking me to a couple of local places. I also have an old friend in town that I have been spending time with, so I think I'm really going to like it here."

"So, what can I do for you today?" Steph took a seat behind the desk, crossing her legs and shifting a stack of paperwork to better see Kerri.

"I was hoping that it would be okay if I left the office for a couple of hours. I have everything well in hand here and I wanted to take some time to snap a few stock photos for several stories that I have on the backburner." Kerri shifted uncomfortably in her seat, she hated to ask, but sitting around a quiet newsroom only left more time for her to dwell on the message she had received from Summer.

"I think that is a wonderful idea. Plus, it is a beautiful day and lord knows I would be trying to find a way out of this office if I wasn't drowning in paperwork." Steph smiled.

"That's great!" Kerri jumped from the chair and tossed her bag back over her head. "Thanks, Steph. I will have my phone with me so you can reach me if I'm needed. Otherwise, I will be back in a little while."

Kerri practically jogged down the hall at the prospect of getting out of the office and into the fresh air. Her mood was short lived, however, as she stepped into the street to catch a glimpse of Doug walking into the office of the boutique hotel next to The Little Café across the street. He was holding the hand of a woman, and Kerri's heart sunk when she assumed it was Summer.

Kerri gasped as the woman turned to look at Doug and she realized that it was a different brunette fawning over him and wordlessly flirting. Her guilt about Summer lessened a little with the thought that Doug may also be having an affair. And then that word started to repeat over and over again in her head. Affair. She was having an affair with a married woman.

Kerri felt the vomit rise in her throat as she tried to shake the word from her head. She suddenly remembered the camera hanging around her neck and worked quickly to try and capture Doug and the woman he was with as they lingered in the office window. The glare from the glass made it impossible to see her face, but Kerri waited out of sight for the pair to exit so she could try to get a better shot.

A few minutes later she watched as the clerk handed Doug a white card and he and the woman turned to leave the office. Kerri took close to a hundred photos as they walked in front of the building and opened the door to one of the rooms on the ground floor. Her heart raced with adrenaline and her feet kept pace as she turned and made her way back to the office to get a look at the images.

Kerri plugged her camera into her computer and found the best photo of the woman's face before grabbing her cell phone and dialing Summer's number. She looked at the digits on the screen but cleared them back again, remembering that Summer had asked her not to contact her. Instead, she picked up her work phone and dialed.

Summer picked up after a couple of rings. "Hello?"

"Hey, I know you told me not to contact you, but I have something that you need to see. Is there any chance you can get away? Say you have to meet a client or something and come over to the Observer office?"

"Not right away. I can be there in about an hour. You'll still be around?"

"I'll wait. Just get here as soon as you can." Kerri hung up the phone and started to flick through the other photos she had taken that afternoon to waste time before Summer arrived.

Kerri was engrossed in organizing her stock photos when Julia popped her head around the corner of her cubical, "You have a visitor. One Miss Summer is here to see you."

Kerri jumped to her feet, "can you send her in, or do I have to go meet her?"

"I'll send her in. Don't say I don't do anything for you!" Julia smiled and tapped the edge of the cubical door before disappearing back down the hall.

Kerri fussed with the papers on her desk and put her camera back in the bag before giving herself a once over in anticipation of Summer walking through the door. She stood from the desk and paced the room before deciding to sit back behind the computer and try to look casual.

Summer tapped gently on the doorframe before entering Kerri's office. "Hey! I got here as soon as I could. What's so important that you had to see me in the middle of the day?"

Kerri took a deep breath and opened the photo of Doug and the mystery woman on her screen. "This. Come take a look."

Summer's puzzled expression turned to one of surprise. "Am I seeing what I think I'm seeing?"

"I didn't know how else to tell you and have you believe me. I saw them at the hotel across the street. I think Doug is having an affair. I took a ton of photos; I wasn't sure if you would believe me otherwise."

Summer slumped into the chair across from Kerri. "I would have noticed, wouldn't I? He isn't very good at keeping secrets. He does play an awful lot of poker with the guys..."

"I know you say you are going to leave him, but this has to be the final nail. He doesn't have to know anything else other than you caught him cheating. Now you can leave him without having to explain or without anyone else judging you. And there's no way that he would win a custody fight if this is the reason you file for divorce, is there?"

Summer pulled herself back onto her feet. "Yeah. No judgment now. I, ah, I have to get back to work. I'll talk to you soon." She turned without giving Kerri a chance to speak and left the building.

Kerri checked her watch, 4:50 and almost time to call it a day. She fussed with the papers on her desk and reorganized her drawers before calling the Chinese food place down the block for a takeout order. "I really should go grocery shopping." She muttered as she hung up the phone, grabbed her coat and started the walk to the restaurant.

Kerri finished doing the supper dishes and pulled the whiskey bottle from the cabinet. She lifted it to her eye line and realized there was only a shot or two left in the bottle. She grabbed her jacket from the closet to head to the liquor store and opened the door to find Summer, hand ready to knock, in the doorway of Kerri's apartment.

"I was just on my way out for a minute. Do you have much time?" Kerri stepped back to invite Summer in.

"I can wait if you want."

"I just have to run across the street to the store. Should be five minutes. Make yourself at home." Kerri smiled and closed the door behind her.

Summer puttered around Kerri's apartment. She noticed that Kerri had added a few personal touches to the place, a photo of Jack, Martha, and the kids, a picture of Kerri, Jack, and their parents on a family vacation when they were young and a small photo of her and Kerri from Kerri's 19th birthday party sat by the stereo. Summer replaced the photo on the shelf as Kerri opened the door, paper bag in hand.

Kerri threw her jacket over the back of a chair and headed to the kitchen with the bottle. "Can I offer you a drink?" She hollered back over her shoulder.

"I'm fine. Well, water if you wouldn't mind."

Kerri poured her whiskey and filled a larger glass with water for Summer, presenting it to her and gesturing for them to take a seat on the couch. "Sorry I ran out like that. I wasn't expecting to see you tonight. What's up?"

"I couldn't face him. I don't know how to say it is over and have that be true. I have tried before and he just tells me that I'm being immature and foolish, and I don't leave. And he threatened again to fight for Ava. I think that's the worst part about all this. I know the court tends to side with the mother and as a lawyer I know that he doesn't have much of a case, but it still scares me to have to go through that, to have to put Ava through it." Summer buried her face in her hands.

Kerri downed her drink and stood up from the couch.

"So… you are here, in my apartment looking for me to console you because you can't leave your husband? That's fucked up, Summer." All the anger and frustration that Kerri had been feeling started to boil over inside her.

"I'm not saying I can't. I'm just saying that I'm afraid. Even with the photos that you showed me, I don't know if I'm strong enough to be on my own." Summer stood and moved toward Kerri, resting her cheek against Kerri's chest and shoulder.

Kerri pushed her away. "Don't expect me to comfort you. You come here looking for what? Affection? Love? Sex?" Kerri took another step back and folded her arms across her chest. "Not anymore. I'm not going to be the second choice. I'm not going to hide in the shadows to leave the house with you. I'm not going to pretend I'm someone I'm not for other people. If you want to be with me, you can leave him. That's it. I get that Ava is complicating things for you, but you just said yourself that he wouldn't win."

"I'm not asking you to hide who you are. And I'm not saying that I won't leave him!" Summer shouted. "You are not my second choice," her voice softened, "You mean everything to me."

"Prove it. I want you to leave." Kerri moved toward the door, swinging it open. "Please. Just get out. Leave me alone until you are ready to be with only me. I can't deal with the guilt anymore."

Summer stood in the entranceway. "I love you. You just have to give me a little more time."

"I can't keep waiting for you. I have been waiting for you since the moment we met. If you leave him, come talk to me. Until then, I don't want to see or hear from you again. Goodbye, Summer." Kerri closed the door.

CHAPTER 17

Kerri was in a funk all throughout the day on Friday. She was conflicted about the argument she had with Summer the night before, having blurted out many of the things she was feeling, but not really meaning to have said them out loud. She avoided conversations with her coworkers as much as possible and even ate her lunch in her car to avoid Julia. She submitted her final assignment by midafternoon and watched the clock tick away the hours until she would finish her first week at her new job.

Kerri logged off her computer a couple of minutes before five, hoping to avoid seeing anyone when she left for the weekend. She was torn between wanting to talk to someone about the fight and wanting to spend time alone wallowing in self-pity about it. She turned her head at the sound of cheering from a nearby office and walked directly into Julia.

"Well that's one way to get a girl's attention!" Julia staggered back, catching herself on the front desk.

"Sorry. I was distracted; I didn't even see you there." Kerri blushed. "Are you hurt?"

"Just my pride. I'll be fine. Haven't seen much of you over the past couple of days. Got plans for the weekend?"

Kerri shook her head. "Nah, you are pretty much the only person I know around here. I thought I might head back to Jenkinstown for the weekend, but there is nothing going on at home, so I'll probably just watch a marathon of *Buffy* or something."

Julia laughed, "That sounds like a great weekend, don't suppose you would mind some company?"

Kerri blushed and brushed her bang out of her eyes. "Ah, no, I, ah, suppose that would be alright. I was going to head home and get started, but I don't really have anything to offer you to eat. It's been a weird week and I haven't really picked up any groceries since moving in."

"I was going to hit La Bistro for dinner and a drink, if you want to join. You could always grab your DVDs and we could watch at my place; I live right above the restaurant." Julia swallowed hard and felt the palms of her hands start to sweat.

"That actually sounds really cool. We can pick favourites from every season to watch. I'll head to the apartment and pick up the box set and meet you at the restaurant in twenty?" Kerri ran her hand along the back of her neck, suddenly nervous about going to dinner.

Julia wiped her hands on the front of her pants and shifted her weight awkwardly to lean against the desk. "Perfect! It's a date." She pushed herself upright and hustled down the hall to her office to gather her things.

Kerri dashed out into the hall, her face flush and her heart racing. She hoped she had not given Julia the wrong impression, but she had called it a date. Kerri paused to wonder if it should be a date, she had told Summer not to come back until she left Doug and Kerri wasn't holding out hope that it would happen. Kerri knew she wasn't ready to move on, but she really liked the attention that

Julia gave her, and it would be nice to get to know her better.

Julia was already seated at a table in the back corner with two glasses of whiskey in front of her when Kerri arrived at La Bistro. Kerri sat and Julia pushed one of the glasses in her direction. "I hope you didn't think I was double fisting. Also, I'm sorry if I assumed with the order."

"No, no. This is perfect. Thanks. So, about tonight…" Kerri stumbled over the words.

"Yeah, I realized what I said. I didn't really mean a date. I get that you are hung up on Summer. I was actually wondering why you weren't spending tonight with her? Especially after she showed up to see you at work the other day."

Kerri sighed. "I don't know if I'm going to see her again." Their food arrived and Kerri filled Julia in on all the drama they had managed to squeeze into the last week as they ate. "I'm not sure if I should hold out hope or not."

"Sounds like you guys are acting like a couple of teenagers. I haven't had to deal with that much drama from a girl in a long time." Julia mused and gestured at the waitress to bring them another drink.

"Well, there is a lot of history there. We were just kids when we got together the first time. I think we could figure out how to be together as adults, but not with all the jealously and obstacles we are dealing with right now. I just needed to take a step back from it all. I'm willing to work at it, but not until she doesn't have a husband waiting at home."

"That just makes sense. I tried to get back together with a girl I dated in high school once." Julia chuckled.

Kerri raised an eyebrow, "I have a feeling you are going to tell me that it didn't go very well?"

"The sex was amazing, but she got immediately attached like we were in a relationship after one night and started following me around like a lovesick teenager. When I really thought about it, that was why I broke up with her to begin with. She was way too clingy. Not that I think that's the problem in this case." Julia backtracked.

"It's cool. I didn't read anything into it." Kerri finished her drink just in time for the waitress to return with their refills. "I am, however, starting to think that you are trying to get me drunk."

"I would never!" Julia gasped. "Just making sure that you are keeping up with me."

"Alright. So, tell me more about you?" Kerri slumped down in her seat, full from her meal, and sipped on her whiskey.

"Not much to tell really. I'm from here, went to college here, got a job here and now we are here." Julia joked.

"I guess that is putting it concisely." Kerri slammed her empty glass upside down on the table. "And I guess that's it for me for the moment. You wanna get this marathon started?"

Julia tipped back her glass, finishing the rest of her drink. "Yeah. Let's head out."

They each paid their tab and stepped out the front door of the restaurant. Kerri hung back a little, waiting for directions as Julia turned to the very next door and headed up the stairs. Kerri followed cautiously behind as Julia unlocked the door at the top of the steps and opened it to reveal a huge living space with a short set of stairs leading to a pair of doors on one side of the foyer and an open area with 16 foot ceilings on the other side.

"Wow. This is quite the place." Kerri looked around at the ornate decoration in the stairwell with more modern touches in the open concept living room, dining room and kitchen area. "I guess I didn't expect anything so grand to be located above a restaurant."

"Oh, yeah. It's okay I guess." Julia blushed, embarrassed by Kerri's reaction. "Can I offer you a drink? I know I have a bottle of whiskey here somewhere." She made her way to the kitchen and opened a cupboard to reveal a fully stocked liquor cabinet.

"Whatever is easy will be fine." Kerri pulled the *Buffy* box set from her bag and placed it on the coffee table in front of the television. "Got a particular episode you want to start with?"

"I'm always good to start with the musical." Julia giggled, placing a pair of glasses and an unopened bottle of whiskey on the table beside the DVDs. "Figured I would bring the whole bottle, keep us from having to pause and get up."

Kerri could already feel the warmth in her cheeks from the several drinks she had over dinner. Despite her better judgment, she poured herself another drink while Julia popped the DVD in the player and grabbed the remote before flopping down on the couch beside her. Kerri listened for the familiar sound of the wolf howl as the main menu loaded.

"I have to warn you, I'm probably going to sing along... and I have been known to recreate the dance moves from some of the scenes." Kerri blushed.

"I hope you don't think you are the only one! It is sacrilege not to sing along!" Julia laughed and pressed play.

They laughed and chatted, pointing out their favourite parts of the show and putting a good dent in the bottle of whiskey as they sang along. The episode was nearing the end when they found themselves facing each other, holding hands and singing to one another. The music swelled as Buffy and Spike shared a kiss before the curtain and Kerri didn't stop it as Julia leaned in and kissed her in the same moment.

Kerri felt the cool sensation of her lips from the ice in Julia's glass and the softness of her hand as it landed against Kerri's neck. Kerri surprised herself by leaning into the kiss and placing one hand on Julia's hip and running the other along the back of her neck and into her hair. She shivered as Julia grabbed the tail of her shirt and twisted it in her fingers.

Kerri allowed the fog of the whiskey to take over and the longing for attention from someone that didn't also bring a lot of complications to be in control. She pressed harder into the kiss, forcing Julia to let go of her shirt to balance herself on the couch. Julia pulled her hand down from Kerri's neck, resting it on her chest, just above her heart. She used the other hand to grasp on to Kerri's waist and pull her closer before slipping it under the edge of her shirt, along her hip and onto her lower back.

Julia allowed her fingertips to trail up Kerri's spine and she was about to undo her bra when Kerri pulled back suddenly, jumping from the couch and almost falling over the coffee table. "I'm – I'm so sorry. I don't know what came over me."

Julia smiled. "Take a breath. It's okay. I started it."

"But I let you, and I let it continue and I can't do this. I shouldn't be here." Kerri stopped, looking down at Julia. "I'm in love with someone else. Maybe we aren't together right now, but I can't lead you on. I may have been kissing you just now, but I wasn't thinking about you and that isn't fair."

"Woah, slow down Kerri. You think I don't know that?" Julia stood in front of Kerri. "I'm not asking you for anything, okay? We were having fun, it seemed like a moment and I didn't want to let it pass without seeing what would happen."

"I, ah, I should go. I'm so, so sorry. Can we just pretend that it never happened? I could really use a friend." The fog of the alcohol was lifting with the adrenaline racing through Kerri.

"It's cool, really. I understand and we can most definitely be friends. You don't have to leave. I promise not to kiss you again."

"No, it's getting late anyway, and I think I need to apologize to Summer, if she'll talk to me." Kerri grabbed her jacket and headed out of Julia's apartment before taking out her cell phone and dialing Summer's number.

It was a little late to call, but she didn't want to wait until the morning to take back the things she had said the night before. Julia had been right when she said they were acting like kids about their relationship, fighting over nothing and making a big deal out of little things. The phone rang for the third time when a man's voice came on the line.

"Hello? Can I help you?"

Kerri froze, unsure if she should hang up or respond before managing to croak out a few words. "Can I speak to Summer?"

"This is her husband; can I help you?" Doug replied firmly.

Kerri took a deep breath, puffing out her chest. "No, you can't. I need to speak to Summer."

"Summer can't talk right now. There was, ah, an accident and she is in the hospital." He replied.

"Oh my god! What happened? Is she okay? I'll come see her. Where is she?" The questions poured out of Kerri without thinking.

"The police are investigating, and they don't know if she is going to be alright or not at this point. She's in critical condition and unconscious. This is Kerri, isn't it?" Doug's voice lowered as he asked.

"Yes. I'm heading to the hospital now. What room is she in?" Kerri picked up the pace and scanned the street for a taxi.

"Don't even think about coming here. I know what you are doing with my wife and it is disgusting. I don't want to see your face and I don't want you coming anywhere near her again, you understand me? If you show up, you're going to get more than you bargained for." Doug threatened.

Kerri felt the anger swell inside her. "You listen to me. I am not afraid of you. She would want me to be there. I'm coming, whether you like it or not." Kerri closed the phone and checked the time, just after midnight. She called the only number she had for a cab and sat on a bus bench to wait.

There was a lump in her throat as she pushed through the emergency doors of the hospital and made her way to the closest nurse's station. Kerri tapped her fingers on the top of the desk as she waited for the man standing in scrubs, making notes on a patient chart, to notice her. She cleared her throat to get his attention and he frowned as he put the clip board down and made his way over.

"What can I do for you tonight, miss?" He forced a smile.

"My, ah, friend was brought in earlier tonight. She

was in an accident? I need to know what room she's in."

"Name?"

"Kerri Walters," she replied and watched as he typed it into the computer. "No, that's my name, hers is Summer. Summer Donnelly... Peters."

The nurse huffed and cleared the screen to search again. "Second floor ICU, but they may not let you in."

Kerri was already off and running down the hall to the stairwell. "Thanks," she waved behind her and she bounded up the two flights of stairs, holding her breath.

Kerri skidded to a halt outside the glass of Summer's room. Doug was sitting facing the bed, leaned back in his chair, arms folded across his chest. He seemed to be speaking, but Kerri couldn't hear the words and the chair blocked her view of Summer's face. She could hear her heart beating in her ears from the run up the stairs and struggled to catch her breath before opening the door.

Doug stood from his seat and their eyes met through the glass that separated the room from the hall. His hands were balled into fists at his side as he marched toward her. Kerri's hands were shaking but she stood her ground as he walked up to her and stopped just inches from her face.

"I warned you not to show your face around here. I have enough to handle without having to deal with some dyke that is trying to steal my wife and break up my family. You can leave now, or I will call security."

"Go ahead, call them. I'm not leaving." Kerri folded her arms across her chest and widened her stance. "I'll have you know that I'm not trying to break anyone up. She came to me. She says she never should have married you and that you know it. Besides, I know damn well that you are having a little thing of your own. I saw you with that woman and I got evidence, so Summer knows it too."

"Doug, Doug, we're here. How is she?" A familiar voice carried down the hallway toward them. "Oh my, Kerri? Is that you?"

Kerri smiled coyly. Summer's mother had always been fond of her and she spent many afternoon's chatting with Eileen across their front yard. "Joan! So nice to see you, I wish it was under better circumstances."

Joan was carrying baby Ava and passed her off to Doug to pull Kerri into an embrace. "Have you seen her yet? She always asks about you. Sum would be so glad that you came." Joan ran her hands over the front of her skirt, wiping away the wrinkles. "I went to pick up Ava from the sitter, has there been any change?"

"I only just arrived. Do you know what happened?"

Joan shook her head and slowly exhaled. "Only that they found her in an alley and that she had been beaten pretty badly. It's hard to see her like this, but my girl is a tough one. I know she'll pull through." Joan took Kerri by the hand and walked her into the room.

Kerri's breath caught in her throat as she saw the tube coming from Summer's mouth. There was a gash across her cheek, her nose appeared to be broken and her head was wrapped in a bandage. Kerri's knees were weak, barely holding her on her feet but she couldn't look away. If she had ever had any doubt that Summer was the love of her life, this moment carried it away on the wind.

Kerri coughed, holding back a sob as Joan smiled at her. "She is stable, but critical. Doctors say it is a waiting game because they don't know the extent of the damage from the head injury." Joan looked over at Summer and back to Kerri, squeezing her hand. "I'm so glad you are here, honey."

Kerri forced a smile. "It's okay if I stay with her for a while?" She sat in the chair beside the bed and held Summer's hand.

"Of course, dear. Stay as long as you want. I'm going to send Doug home with the baby and head downstairs and get some tea, would you like anything?"

"No, I'm okay. Thank you, though." Kerri held Summer's limp hand between hers and pressed her lips to the back of her fingers. She waited until Joan was out of the room before she finally allowed a sob to escape her throat.

"Come on Sum, you have to wake up. I need you. I shouldn't have said any of those things last night. I know that you want to be with me. I love you more than I even realized until I saw you in this bed. I can't live without you. You have to wake up and tell me that you still love me too, even after our fight. You have to. Please?" Kerri pleaded with the unconscious girl. She was suddenly exhausted and linked her pinky into Summer's before leaning back and falling asleep in the chair.

CHAPTER 18

Kerri woke suddenly and glanced around the room unsure of her surroundings until her eyes landed on Summer and the events of the night before came flooding back. She had been stirred by the sound of hushed voices in the room and pulled down a blanket that someone had placed over her during the night. She stretched and rubbed her neck, sore from sleeping sitting up, and looked around to see Joan speaking with a nurse and a uniformed police officer.

"Oh, honey, you're awake. I'm sorry if we disturbed you. I covered you up, you looked like you might be cold. It's very sweet that you spent the night." Joan patted her on the shoulder.

Kerri rubbed her eyes trying to remember everything that happened the night before. She had barely asked any questions about the attack, but the only person she really wanted to hear it from was Summer, and she was going to be answering anytime soon. "Thank you, for the blanket. I couldn't figure where else I should be, so I stayed with her. I came the second I heard. When did it happen? It couldn't have been last night if you're already in town."

Joan sat on the edge of the hospital bed in front of Kerri. "It was Thursday night. She is one tough cookie, police found her because she tried to call 9-1-1 while she was being attacked. It was just after 11 when we got the call that she was here."

"And, where did you say she was attacked?" Kerri had switched to interview mode, removing herself from the answers to keep her composure.

"Umm, I believe they said she was behind some club, but it sounds more like a clothing store to me, something called The Closet?"

Kerri stifled a laugh. "It's a club alright, but I can't understand what she would have been doing there. I had just seen her a little earlier that night and she didn't say anything about going to a bar, especially that one. It just doesn't make any sense."

The police officer perked up. "You saw her, on Thursday night? The night she was attacked? Your name?"

Kerri nodded. "Kerri Walters. She came by my apartment unannounced. I had been drinking a little and we had a stupid fight. I would never have known she was in the hospital if I didn't call last night to try to apologize and Doug answered the phone."

"And what was the argument about?" The officer replied.

"It was personal and has nothing to do with this, I can assure you."

"All the same, please answer the question. You can cooperate here, or I can take you down to the station for more questioning. You've already admitted that the two of you fought, so I have cause."

Kerri shot a sideways glance at Joan and took a deep breath. "We fought about her husband, Doug."

The officer jotted something on his note pad. "And what about him, exactly, caused you to fight?"

"I'd really rather not say." Kerri glanced at Joan again, biting her lower lip.

"Again, Ms. Walters, we can do this at the station." He tapped his pen against the pad in his hand.

"I told Summer that I didn't want to see her anymore unless she left him." Kerri blurted out as quickly and with as little detail as possible.

The officer made another note. "So, you have a problem with her husband? You want to tell me why?"

"No, well, I don't really have a problem with him personally, I mean, we don't know each other. He probably has a problem with me personally, but that's my own fault. I mean, it wasn't really about him, it was about her being with him." Kerri couldn't help but ramble.

"Umhm, I see. Let me ask you this another way. What is your relationship to Mrs. Peters?"

Kerri's stomach rolled and beads of sweat formed on her forehead and the back of her neck. She brushed her bang out of her eyes and struggled to find the right words. "Relationship?" She managed to choke. "We're old friends who had been spending a lot of time together lately."

"So, it wasn't because you were jealous of Mr. Peters that you had the argument?"

"No, I mean, yes, I mean, sort of. Do you really need me to get into this any further?" Kerri shifted her weight nervously.

The officer furrowed his brow. "I just want a clear answer as to what your relationship is to the victim. You were the last person to talk to her before the attack, she showed up at your house…" he tapped his note pad, "unannounced, late in the evening on Thursday and you fought about her husband. I'm just trying to determine that you don't have a motive in this case."

Kerri's eyes widened. "I most certainly do not. I was jealous, but not because I have any interest in him. I'm in love with her, and she says she feels the same, and she showed up, but she was still with him and we fought about it." Panic rose in Kerri's chest as she blurted out the words and realized that Joan heard every one.

Joan moved over beside Kerri and wrapped her arm around her shoulders. "I always thought there was something between you two, you know. You were so close when we lived next door and I was really just waiting for you guys to tell me you were together, especially after the time you hurt your knee. But then she decided to move for school and met Doug, so I figured I was wrong."

"She told me she couldn't do it back then. She broke my heart." Tears started to fall down Kerri's face and Joan pulled her in, letting her cry against her shoulder. "She says she isn't happy and that she finally wants us to be together and now I don't know if she will even wake up. I shouldn't have told you, though. It wasn't my place."

Joan looked over at her daughter, struggling for life on a ventilator. "I don't think she will mind. If any of this can help with the investigation, I'm sure that she isn't going to care one bit."

Kerri sniffed and looked back at the officer. "I told her to leave and not to come back until she had ended it with Doug. I have no idea where she went or what happened after that. I wish I hadn't said it. I wish I could take it back. That's exactly what I was trying to do when I called last night. I don't know if any of this is a help."

The officer scribbled a little more on his pad before sliding it and his pen back into his pants pocket. "Actually, it does help. It helps to establish the timeline of where she was before she called 9-1-1 from that alley. She fought back. We got skin scrapings from under her fingernails but no DNA match in the system. We do know that she was attacked by a man, so I don't expect you will have to answer any further questions but take my card just in case you remember anything else. Even the smallest detail could help establish where she was headed. Thank you for your time, Ms. Walters, and I'm sorry." He tipped his hat and left the room.

"Now, honey, you know how tough my daughter is better than anyone." Joan smiled at her, hugging her again. "We are just going to get through the waiting together."

Doug returned to the hospital later that afternoon and Kerri decided to use the opportunity to head home, shower, get a change of clothes and cook a meal for Joan. She didn't want to leave, but she couldn't handle the angry eyes and the hard looks she was getting from Doug. Kerri returned to the room just after seven that evening, and Doug had already left again.

"He said he had to go home with Ava. I guess the babysitter could only stay for a couple of hours. We got an update from the doctor." Joan took Kerri by the hands.

"Please say that its good news, or that they at least have a better idea of what is going on."

"It is good. The new scans came back and they are completely confident that she is going to wake up, it is just a matter of time. The swelling is down in her brain and they're hopeful that she will be back with us in the next couple of days."

"That's amazing," Kerri grabbed Joan into a hug and pulled her off the ground in her excitement. "Does Doug know?" Kerri choked on the words.

"He was here when the doctor came in. Actually, he left right after we got the prognosis. I guess that's what he was waiting around for."

"You should call it a night. I made you a plate. I know it isn't much, but you have to keep your strength up. I'll take the night shift and you can go get some rest." Kerri passed a plastic container to Joan and took her place in the chair beside the bed.

"Don't you have to work tomorrow? I can stay."

Kerri shook her head. I sent my boss an email and explained what was going on. That woman must be glued to her computer because she got back to me almost immediately. I'm going to take the mid-day shift for at least tomorrow and Monday, so I don't have to go in until after lunch."

Kerri made herself as comfortable as possible in the chair and linked her pinky into Summer's as she listened to the sound of the machine that was helping Summer breathe. She hummed absentmindedly, her thoughts going back to the night she had hurt her knee and the songs she had sung to herself as she hoped for someone to come and help her. The music had been comforting to her as it reminded her of Summer, and she hoped it would help to bring her back to consciousness.

Kerri woke with an ache in her neck and back. She had spent another night sleeping in the chair beside Summer's bed. The nurse was checking Summer's vitals and fluids and laughed when she heard Kerri groan. "We should put a cot in here for you. This is the second morning I have found you here at the start of my shift. Let me check around and see if I can get one for tonight, okay?"

Kerri smiled. "I really just don't want to leave, in case she wakes up, you know? I have to be here when she wakes up." She picked up Summer's hand and stroked it gently, "Come on Sum, it's time to get up."

Joan clasped her hand on Kerri's shoulder, hearing her pleading words. "Good morning, honey. How is our girl doing?" Kerri went to speak, but Joan cut her off. "I was talking to Summer. Did you get any sleep at all?"

"A little. I must have dozed off at some point." Kerri said, rubbing her neck and getting out of the chair to stretch the rest of her body.

Kerri's phone vibrated in her pocket and she excused herself to answer it. "Kerri Walters."

"Hey Ker, Julia. Its work related I promise. I just got word that there was another killing last night, and the police have more information, so they are holding a press conference at noon. I know you switched shifts, but it is our story, if you want to be there."

"Yeah, for sure. I'll be there." Kerri held her breath, "It wasn't about you, the shift switching, in case you thought it was." There was silence on the line. Kerri looked at the phone to see if the call was still connected. "Julia?"

"It's fine. I'm sorry for the other night. I just hope we can still be friends and that working together isn't going to be weird."

"Don't give it another thought. We're cool. I promise. I'll see you this afternoon." Kerri snapped the phone closed and went back to Summer's side to explain the situation to Joan. Kerri was more invested than ever in the case as Summer had been attacked in the same alley where the previous murders were thought to have taken place.

Kerri left the hospital with enough time to swing by her apartment and freshen up before the press conference. Julia was waiting for her outside the police station when she arrived. "Hey, am I late? It's been a weird couple of days."

"Nope, right on time. We can talk about it after, if you want?"

"Maybe. Let's get in there." Kerri pulled open the door and found her usual set up spot near the front of the room was taken, so she pulled out her camera and started to plan a moving approach. The last of the journalists were just taking their seats when the Police Chief entered and made his way to the podium. This was getting to be an all too familiar scene for Kerri.

"Good afternoon ladies and gentlemen. As you know, you are here so we can provide an update on the ongoing investigation surrounding a series of murders near a local club. On Saturday night, yet another body was found. A 25-year-old woman that we believe is also connected to this case. We have received a number of leads from the public after the release of the sketch from a witness last week, but we have yet to make any arrests." There was a grumbling in the crowd.

"I also wanted to say that we believe we may have another eyewitness. A woman was found beaten in the same alley on Thursday of last week. Although she had not yet regained consciousness, she is expected to wake soon, and we are hoping she will be able to provide us with more information about her attacker. These attacks are becoming more frequent so we believe the killer is no longer able to control his urges and could strike again soon. We are asking folks to travel in pairs at night, and to avoid poorly lit areas. In the meantime, we are encouraging anyone who believes they may have information related to the case to come forward and contact police. Help us make our community safe once again. Thank you."

The chief didn't wait around for questions this time, but simply walked away from the microphone and through a curtain at the back of the room. Kerri stood, completely still, unable to move or speak. The police had now confirmed her fear, they thought that whatever happened to Summer was connected to the serial killings. Julia approached, tapping her on the shoulder.

"You ready to go?" She looked at Kerri, concerned.

Kerri hadn't blinked, her mouth still hung agape after hearing the words. Her feet were frozen to the ground and she couldn't bring herself to release her breath. Kerri could hear Julia speaking to her, but she wasn't able to respond. It had been difficult to see Summer in that hospital bed, but she hadn't allowed any of it to sink in until she heard the officer basically say that Summer was lucky to be alive.

"Kerri? Earth to Kerri?" Julia snapped her fingers in front of Kerri's eyes, causing her to finally blink.

"Yeah, yeah, let's go," Kerri stuttered.

Kerri had walked to the station and accepted a ride from Julia back to the office. On the drive, she explained her reaction at the press conference. "Sorry I zoned out on you back there. The woman that was beaten and survived?"

"What about her?"

"It was Summer. It must have happened after I kicked her out of my place the other night."

Julia swerved the car as she turned to look at Kerri before quickly correcting the wheel. "What? That's not possible."

"It's the truth. I've spent the past couple of nights at the hospital, but there has been no change."

"Is there anything you can do, anything you can tell them about that night that will help?"

"I told them everything I could. Now we wait. You heard the officer. We just need her to wake up and tell us all what happened. I just want to get through today so I can be back with her, you know?"

"For sure. Let's put this story to bed so you can." Julia pulled the car into the underground parking at the Observer and they entered in silence.

CHAPTER 19

Kerri woke with a start and slowly pulled herself into a more seated position as she rubbed her eyes and tried to figure out where she was. The now familiar beeping of the hospital monitors brought her back to reality as she released her grip on Summer's hand. She had fallen asleep in the chair by her bedside for the third night in a row.

Joan was seated across from her reading but looked up from the page when Kerri started to move. "Did you sleep okay? You really can't be getting much rest in that chair."

"I'm good. A little achy, but good. Still no sign of Doug?"

"No. He wasn't by at all yesterday and I can't reach him to see if he will be here today. I'm going to head out and pick up Ava for a couple of hours. She has been spending too much time with the sitter through all of this."

"Sure thing. I'll stay a while longer."

Kerri was able to relax a little more now that Summer was breathing on her own. The doctors had come by and removed the ventilator not long after she arrived that previous evening. Kerri also felt a little more relaxed with the police officer that was posted in the hallway. There were concerns for Summer's safety since the press conference made it public knowledge that she was expected to recover from the attack. The police were concerned the suspect could get into her room and finish the job before she was able to tell them what happened and give a description of her attacker.

Kerri curled her legs up into the chair and looked at the cot that had been moved into the room. She was exhausted and knew that she needed to get at least a couple of real hours of sleep. She squeezed Summer's hand and pulled the cot as close to the side of her bed as she could before crawling in and closing her eyes again.

Kerri woke to the sound of her name being whispered softly. She rolled over to see Summer looking her in the eyes. Kerri gasped, "Sum? You're – you're awake!" Kerri jumped off the cot and sat herself on the edge of Summer's bed, grabbing her by the hand.

"Kerri, I'm so happy you're here. I, my face hurts." Summer touched the bandages around her nose and grimaced when her fingers brushed over the cut on her cheek.

Kerri couldn't help but laugh. "I bet it does. Do you remember what happened?"

"Bits and pieces. I remember that I came to see you." Summer cringed in pain as she tried to turn her head more to face Kerri.

"Hold that thought. There is someone else who is going to want to hear this." Kerri ran into the hall and returned with the police officer that had been standing guard.

"Nice to have you back with us, Mrs. Peters. Your friend says you are ready to talk about what happened?"

"I think so. My head is killing me, but I'll do my best. And please, call me Summer." She gripped Kerri's hand

and took a deep breath.

Kerri squeezed her hand in return. "It's okay love, take your time."

"So, I left Kerri's apartment on Thursday evening and was planning to take a walk to calm down. I hadn't gone very far when I thought I saw my husband walking with a woman up ahead. I was almost certain that he was having an affair, so I decided to follow him to confront him. I kept my distance for a while, until they picked up the pace and ducked in behind the buildings and down the back alley. I moved faster to get to them and saw that he had her pinned against the wall. I figured he was making his move." Summer stopped, rubbing her temples.

"Do you want me to get a nurse? See if they can give you something for the pain?" Kerri brushed the back of her fingers across Summer's face.

"Not yet. I want to get this out first."

"So, he had the woman pinned, Mrs... Summer. What happened next?"

"I shouted his name and when he turned to look at me, the woman he was with took off down the alley. I ran toward him, ready to confront him about the affair when I noticed that he had a steal pipe in his hand. I stopped moving and he was just standing there looking at me, but before I knew it, he was on top of me, punching me in the face. I saw him raise the pipe and the next thing I remember is waking up here a little while ago."

"Just to make sure we are clear, you are saying that your husband, Doug Peters is responsible?" The officer placed his hand on his radio, waiting for the confirmation.

"Yes. He is the one who did this to me." Summer confirmed.

The officer depressed the button on the side of his radio, "I have confirmation from the victim. She was assaulted by one Doug Peters. Please send officers to his home and place of business, let's try to make this a quick arrest. I'll be remaining at my post in case he tries to come check on his wife." The officer turned back to Summer, "Can you tell me anything about the other woman? The one that you saw him go into the alley with?"

"Not much, I'm afraid. She was probably about my age, mid 20s with short brown hair and I would guess about 5'6". She was wearing a band t-shirt of Our Lady Peace, maybe? I didn't get a good look at her face."

"Thank you again. You have helped us more than you know." The officer tipped his hat and left the room.

"What does that mean?" Summer turned to Kerri.

Kerri sighed, unsure if she should tell her the connection. "They, the police, well, they think that whoever attacked you is also responsible for The Closet murders."

Summer couldn't speak. She touched the bandages around her head and nodded. Kerri held her hand tighter. "That can't be true. He can't be a killer. There's no way. I have known that man a long time and he would never be able to take another life. Would he?"

Kerri just shook her head. "I don't know. I wish I knew what to say. You said he'd been angrier lately, angry to the point of making you afraid. The police obviously have reasons to think that he is involved, but we just have to wait and see." She yearned to be able to do more to comfort Summer, to be able to hold her and make sure that everything was alright.

"I will be right here, by your side, no matter what happens. I'm sorry. I'm more sorry than I will ever be able to express that I acted like such a child the other night and told you to leave. I didn't really want that, but the thought of you going home to him, sleeping beside him, waking up with him, it was just too much."

"I wasn't going home to him and I certainly wasn't going to sleep beside him. I was going home to my daughter." Summer's expression suddenly changed. "Oh god, Ava. Where is Ava?"

"Your mom is in town. She went to pick her up a little while ago. I expected her to be here by now."

"You have to make sure. Please, she is my whole world. You have to make sure that she is safe." Summer tried to sit up in the bed but grabbed at her head with another burst of pain.

"Just relax. I'll call your mom right now." Kerri pulled the phone from her pocket and searched through her contacts for the number. She paced the floor as she hit send and waited for Joan to answer. "Joan? It's Kerri. Is Ava with you?" Kerri continue to pace, biting at the tip of her thumb. "Okay, right. You should come down here. Sum is finally awake."

Kerri snapped the phone closed and moved back to the chair where she had spent the last couple of nights. "Your mom picked Ava up from daycare and dropped her at the babysitters half an hour ago. She's going to check to make sure everything is okay and then she is coming to see you." She took Summer by the hand and softly pressed her lips to her knuckles.

Summer breathed a sigh of relief. "Good. Maybe you should get that nurse. My head is pounding, and an Advil wouldn't go astray." She struggled to smile at Kerri through the pain. "Don't let them give me anything stronger, though. I want my mind to be clear."

"Yes, ma'am," Kerri saluted as she headed to the

nurse's station across the hall. She was only gone for a minute, but when she returned Summer's eyes were closed and her breathing had deepened into sleep. Kerri took a small cup with two pills from the nurse and placed it on the bedside table before sitting back in the chair and closing her eyes as well.

Kerri woke as Joan attempted to cover her in a blanket. Kerri smiled when she realized Joan was carrying a baby in her arms. "I'm glad she's safe. This must be little Ava?"

"With the amount of time you have apparently been spending with my daughter over the past couple of weeks, I figured you two were acquainted." Joan offered Ava to Kerri to hold.

Kerri waved her off. "No, there was one evening that I thought Summer was going to bring her along, but that didn't happen. I'm not the greatest with kids."

Joan scoffed. "You are going to have to get over that, honey. Especially if you love my daughter as much as you not only say but have demonstrated that you do. They're a package deal, I'm afraid."

"I'm aware. I just haven't spent much time around kids, other than my niece and nephew. I'll figure it out, just give it time."

"I'm sure you will. She really is a very sweet child. You sure you don't want to hold her?"

"Hi mom." A hushed voice came from the bed. "What are you two talking about?" Summer looked at Kerri with panic in her eyes.

Kerri glanced at Joan, who smiled and sat on the edge of the bed beside her daughter. "Well, I was just explaining to Kerri that if she wants to be a part of your life, she is going to have to get used to holding this child."

Summer still looked confused and Kerri took her hand to reassure her. "You have been unconscious for a couple of days. There was a police officer asking me questions and I kind of blurted some things out. I mean, I can't speak for you and how you feel, or where you think this is going, but," Kerri took a deep breath. "I meant it when I said I love you. I'm in love with you."

Summer's jaw dropped as she glanced between Kerri and her mother. "I don't know if this is the time…"

Kerri smiled, placing her hand on Summer's shoulder. "Your mom was here when I talked to the police. She's been amazing about it, truly."

Joan smiled at the pair. "All I ever wanted was for you to be happy. If being with Kerri makes you happy, then that is exactly what you should do. I think you have a good one here. This girl has barely left your bedside. I don't know if she has slept in days."

"She certainly is something, isn't she? I think this could really make me happy. More than I ever thought I could be." Summer looked into Kerri's eyes. "I love you too. But guys, I'm really tired. Can we talk about this later?"

Kerri smiled, "We can talk about whatever you want, whenever you want." She pulled the cup with the pain medication from the table. "Here, you should take these. It will help you sleep." She turned to Joan, "Are you okay to stay with her for a while? I have to get to work for a couple of hours. I promise, I will be back as soon as I can."

"I'm fine and she is going to be fine. Go on to work. We will be right here when you get back." Joan patted Kerri's cheek and bounced Ava on her hip in Kerri's direction. "Say bye-bye, Auntie Kerri."

CHAPTER 20

Kerri was exhausted and on edge, jumping every time a car door slammed near her. She had nightmares about Doug showing up to steal Ava or to try to kill her and as long as he was on the loose, she wasn't sure she would ever be able to relax. When she wasn't at work, Kerri spent her time at the hospital with Summer. She had avoided talking to her coworkers about what was going on, even Julia hadn't brought it up much, but she wasn't able to avoid her boss who had called her in for a meeting.

Kerri walked from the hospital to the Observer the morning of the meeting, overthinking what Steph would want to see her about. She was standing outside the office and tucking in her shirt when the door opened, startling her. Julia winked at Kerri and tapped her on the shoulder with a smile as she passed. "The boss will see you now."

***

Kerri stepped nervously into the office, hoping the meeting was a check-in and not that the numerous requests and favours she asked for in her first couple of weeks on the job had made a bad impression. "Hi Steph, you asked to see me?"

Steph chuckled. "Have a seat. It's all good stuff, I

swear." Steph waited for Kerri to get settled before continuing. "I just wanted to tell you that we are submitting yours and Julia's collaborative articles on The Closet Murders for a national journalism award. It's a rare honour as we only select a couple of pieces a year for submission."

Kerri's jaw dropped. She had been expecting Steph to give her a lecture about asking to change shifts, coming in late and leaving early when she was only in the job for a short time. She was certainly not expecting to receive this kind of praise from her editor. Kerri shifted uncomfortably in her chair, searching for words.

"I know you have been dealing with some personal things since you started and I also see the commitment you have made to the job, despite those issues and I commend you for it. I want to assure you that we will do what we can to accommodate you going forward as well." Steph extended her hand for Kerri to shake.

"Thank you. I don't know what else to say. Things are hopefully going to be back to normal soon. I really appreciate everything you've done, and I am trying not to let my work suffer." Kerri accepted Steph's extended hand.

"Well, it certainly hasn't so far. Thank you for taking the time to meet with me. Now, get back to work."

Kerri stood from the chair and opened the door to the office. She had been grinning for most of the meeting and couldn't shake it when she found Julia waiting for her in her cubical. Julia was bouncing in front of her and squealing as quietly as she could to keep from disturbing the other reporters.

"Oh, my god, oh my god! Three years, I have been trying to get a big story and now it just fell into my lap. They're making me a senior reporter! Steph said it was way overdue plus the nomination! That's just too good to be true!" Julia hugged Kerri, "It never would have happened without you. Your photos and your suggestions for the story have been amazing."

Kerri broke the hug awkwardly. "It's awesome. But you being recognized is only about you. You deserve all the credit. Don't let anyone tell you otherwise." Kerri moved behind her desk and flopped into her chair.

"You got it. Interested in a drink after work to celebrate?"

"Ah, not tonight. I have to head back to the hospital again. I just can't let her be alone, you know?" Her phone buzzed and she pulled it from her pocket to find a text message from Summer.

Overheard the officer in the hall. It's over. They found him.

Kerri snapped the phone shut. "You're not going to believe this, but I just got us the biggest scoop."

Julia raised her eyebrow, "Oh yeah?"

"Yep. The police have made an arrest. Let's get it up on the website. You can say it is from a source inside the investigation. Make a couple of calls and get an interview set up and if I play my cards right I might be able to get a shot of police bringing in the suspect, but I have to get out of here right now."

"Go, go, go. Call me and let me know how it goes. I'll post the article and get the confirmation to go with the photo. See you shortly."

Kerri grabbed her camera and ran out the door. She knew the window was small but getting the heads up from Summer gave her a head-start before the rest of the media got wind of the arrest. She parked up in front of the station just as an officer was pulling someone out of the back of a squad car.

Kerri started snapping photos as she ran across the

parking lot, trying to capture the man's face while he kept his chin down and eyes pointed away from her as she approached. This was her only chance to get the shot until he was brought to court where every reporter in town would be waiting.

Kerri was no more than ten feet away, still snapping her camera when an officer started moving toward her, blocking her view and ushering her away. In the same moment the second officer got the man through the door of the station, so whatever she had was what Kerri was going to get. She texted Julia.

Headed back to you now. Any progress on your end?

Kerri jumped back in her car and pulled across her seatbelt when her phone buzzed.

Got the confirmation. Putting the story together now. Get back here and help me put this to bed.

Kerri smiled at her phone. They had beaten everyone else to the punch and for the first time that week she felt safe. Doug was in custody, Summer was healing faster than expected, Ava was with her grandmother, and Kerri didn't have to keep looking over her shoulder. Kerri released a breath that it felt like she had been holding in for days.

After a couple of hours at the office she had a nice selection of photos pieced together for the article that would run the following morning and several more to upload to the Observer website. She was about to call it a night and head to the hospital when Julia appeared in her door.

"Sure you don't want to get that drink? I think we both deserve one." Julia leaned into the door frame and folded her arms across her chest.

"I'm sure. Another time, though." Kerri smiled. Things had not been weird after Julia had kissed her on the weekend and she wasn't sure if it was because they had both let it go, or because she had too much else on her mind.

"Alright, friend. Maybe when that girlfriend of yours is back on her feet we can all hang out. Say hi for me, would you?" Julia said as genuinely as she could.

"Will do. I should get over there." Kerri grabbed her keys and her coat and headed out.

Summer was asleep when she entered the room but stirred enough to smile at her and squeeze her hand when she took her familiar seat at the side of the bed. Kerri tried not to fully disturb her, leaning in and gently pressing her lips to Summer's temple.

Summer groaned and rolled to face Kerri, her eyes still closed. "I'm glad your back. I'm feeling much better. I just want to go home."

"What did the doctor say? Do you know when you are going to be released?" Kerri stroked Summer's hair which was a little matted where the bandage had now been re-moved.

"Maybe tomorrow. They want to keep me under ob-servation for at least another night, especially since I have been sleeping so much. They want to make sure I'm over the concussion. I just want my own bed."

"Soon. But I was thinking, maybe you should come stay with me for a couple of days once you get released? Your mom would probably like to get back to her bed too, and I could easily be the one to take care of you." Kerri had pondered asking her, but in the moment, it just came out as the most natural thing.

"What about Ava? You don't even like kids, and you haven't spent any time around her. Taking care of an in-fant is no walk in the park. I mean, she is with the babysit-ter during the day and I was planning on hiring a nanny to help with the overnights anyway. Don't you think it would be a little too much, having a small child suddenly inserted into your life?"

"I think there is a very good chance that is going to happen soon enough no matter what. She is a part of you and I'm sure that I will love her. I don't hate kids or anything, I'm just not very good with them."

Summer chuckled, opening one eye to look to see if Kerri was being serious. "You mean that, don't you? You'd be willing to take us both in?"

Kerri laughed a little as she sighed. "You have no idea what I would do for you. Close your eyes. You should be resting, not talking. We can argue about this all you want in the morning." Kerri placed another kiss on Summer's temple and sat back in the chair.

"Ker?" Summer mumbled.

"Yeah?" Kerri sat up straighter.

"Will you just hold me for a little while? Just until I go back to sleep?"

"Sure," Kerri smiled and crawled into the hospital bed beside Summer. She pressed her ear to Summer's back, listening to her heartbeat and the sound of her breath as it slowed and they both drifted off.

Kerri woke a couple of hours later, drenched in sweat from the heat of Summer's body in a bed that was far too small for the both of them. Joan was sitting in the chair, rocking Ava and humming softly as Kerri moved as quietly as possible to get up and let Summer rest. Joan smiled at her and placed Ava in a bassinet on the floor.

Kerri glanced at the clock, 10:15. It was late for Joan to visit, especially to have the baby in tow. Kerri rubbed her eyes and motioned for Joan to join her in the hall. "Is anything wrong? Shouldn't you be home in bed?"

"The police are searching the house. After they arrested Doug, they came by with a warrant, trying to find evidence that he was involved in the other murders and that he's not just guilty of beating his wife almost to death. They need to find something that will connect him to the other crimes."

"Wow. Do you think he did it? I mean, the police said it was all connected, but I can't seem to reconcile that Summer would have put that much trust in someone who was capable of that kind of brutality." Kerri rubbed the back of her neck.

"It's possible. I guess we will have to wait and see. I could have hung around and waited, but it was so disruptive for Ava I figured I would bring her around here, in case Sum was awake and felt up to holding her." Joan placed her hand on Kerri's arm. "I guess what she really felt up to was being held."

"I didn't mean to fall asleep. It was just so relaxing to listen to the sound of her breathing and I haven't slept much this week."

"I know honey. You must be so tired. You really should go home and sleep in your own bed for a change. It could really do you some good, especially now that Doug has been arrested."

"I do feel a lot better knowing that he's behind bars. I still don't want to leave her, though. I need to be here to make sure she is okay. She said they might release her tomorrow?" Kerri brushed her bang from her eyes and tucked her hair behind her ears.

"It certainly looks like they will." Joan smiled.

Kerri picked at a loose thread on the blanket, "How long are you planning to stay in town?"

"I hadn't really decided. I mean, I still have some vacation time that I can take if I need to and I know that Summer isn't going to be able to really take care of Ava on her own for a while."

Kerri cut her off, "What if I said that I asked her to stay with me for a few days when she's released?"

"I would say that it is probably going to be more than a few days before she is able to take care of herself. It is a lot to take on, are you sure you can handle it?" Joan frowned.

"I'm positive." Kerri looked over her shoulder at Summer, still sleeping in the bed. "I will spend the rest of my life taking care of her, if she'll let me."

Joan wrapped her arms around Kerri's waist, pressing her face into her chest. "I had a feeling you were going to say that. I'm so glad she has you, Kerri, not just for her sake, but for Ava's and for mine. You are a wonderful girl and I know that you will do everything you can to help her and make her feel safe."

Kerri returned the hug, "I absolutely will." Kerri yawned, "I'm going to sit with her for a while, you should lie down and get some rest while you can."

Joan pulled herself up onto the cot beside the bed and Kerri sat in the chair, rocking Ava's bassinet with her foot. She hummed Godspeed by the Dixie Chicks and knew she could and would do anything to make sure that Ava and Summer were alright.

CHAPTER 21

Kerri woke early and headed to the cafeteria to grab coffee for herself and Joan. She stretched, trying to loosen the tension in her back from sleeping in the chair again. It was getting worse each night and although they had brought in a cot, she had barely used it. She could handle the pain if it meant Summer never woke up alone in the night.

Kerri kept thinking back to the promise that Summer had made the day she had her knee surgery. Summer had said she would be there when she woke up, and had kept her word so Kerri had made a promise of her own that no matter how many nights she spent sleeping sitting up, she would be there each morning when Summer opened her eyes.

Kerri returned with the coffee to find Joan packing up the few things she had brought to the hospital for Summer with Ava in one arm and Summer still sleeping soundly. "Going somewhere?" Kerri asked.

"The doctor just signed the forms. They are letting her go home this afternoon. I wanted to get a head-start on putting things together before she wakes up." Joan shifted Ava on her hip, struggling to push the items into the gym bag.

"Can I take her from you?" Kerri swallowed. She had yet to hold Ava, but she was going to have to get used to it, and now was as good a time as any to begin. She hesitantly reached out her arms and Joan placed Ava in them. Ava immediately started to cry as Kerri held her.

"Bounce her a little, or maybe walk around the room with her. She'll be okay." Joan could see the panic on Kerri's face.

Kerri bounced and walked, allowing Ava to grasp her finger, softly humming Godspeed once again. It was the only song that came to mind when she tried to think of a lullaby. Summer opened her eyes and grinned from ear to ear as she quietly watched Kerri try to settle Ava, who had buried her face in Kerri's shoulder.

"Well, aren't you two sweet." Summer shifted in the bed, rubbing at her temples.

"It feels a little weird." Kerri said, honestly.

"It did for me at first, too. Just keep moving and she'll sleep like that. You maybe should have put something over your shoulder though, the kid's a drooler."

Kerri could already feel the puddle on her shirt. "It's okay. I was due for a clean shirt anyway. Headache still?" Kerri asked as she watched Summer continue to rub her head.

"Just a little one. Nothing like it has been. I'll be okay."

Joan finished placing the items from the small closet into the bag and sat beside Summer on the bed. "I have some great news, honey. You can go home as of this afternoon."

"That's amazing. I was starting to think I was never getting out of this room." Summer glanced between her mother and Kerri, "Mom, can we have a minute?"

"Sure. I'll take Ava over to the nurse's station. They love to fawn over her."

Joan left, closing the door behind her and Kerri took her spot next to Summer on the bed. "Something wrong?" Kerri asked.

"No, but we need to finish the conversation we were having last night, about me staying with you, now that they are officially going to let me out."

"Ah, right. I don't know how you are going to feel about this, but I kinda mentioned it to your mom while you were asleep. She actually thinks it's a good idea."

"You talked to my mom about it?" Summer pulled back a little. "Never mind, that isn't the point. What I was going to say is that you can't possibly take me and Ava into your little apartment. The couch isn't very comfortable, I should know, and we would be on top of each other, especially when the nanny is working."

Kerri started to get flustered, working out ways that there would be enough space before taking a deep breath and trying to remain calm in the conversation. "Well, I'll be gone all day and of course I would be the one to sleep on the couch…"

Summer put up her hand to stop Kerri from speaking. "Let me finish, would you? On the other hand, I have plenty of room at my house, all of Ava's things are there and no one would be worried about invading anyone else's space."

"So, you're saying that you do want my help, but that I should stay with you? Wouldn't that be weird, I mean, me staying in the house where you lived with your husband?" Kerri picked at a loose thread on the blanket again.

"Only if we make it weird. The house was mine long before he lived in it, so it is up to you if you think you can handle it." Summer placed her hand over Kerri's on the bed. "If it helps, we barely even shared a room. He constantly fell asleep in the den and once Ava was born, he stayed in the guest room so that she wouldn't disturb him if she woke during the night."

Kerri placed her hand on Summer's face, rubbing her thumb along her cheek bone and looking into her eyes, pondering the request. "I can handle it." Kerri felt more confident than ever as she spoke the words.

"Good. Then it is settled. You'll stay at my place until I'm back to myself. And as for where we stand?"

"I don't want to put any pressure on you about that right now. I know that you have been through a lot physically and the emotional backlash hasn't even started yet. Have you even fully absorbed the fact that Doug was arrested? That he is the one who did this to you? Or how about the fact that the police think he might be a serial killer?" Kerri got up from the bed, pacing as Summer spoke.

"It probably hasn't sunk in yet, no. But none of those things are going to change the way that we feel about each other. I just want to make sure that we don't get ahead of ourselves, with you moving in and all."

Kerri huffed. "I'm not moving in. I'm just staying with you to help out until you feel better. There is a big difference. It's not like we were exactly taking it slow before all of this happened, but we shouldn't take me staying with you as anything more than it is."

Summer shook her head, "I suppose you're right. We will have to figure this out as we go. I want you to know that I really appreciate everything that you have been doing and will be doing for me."

Kerri leaned over the bed, kissing Summer on the

cheek. "Don't mention it. Now, let's get you dressed and moving before the doctor shows up to officially release you. I'll get your mom to come in so I can head back to my place and pack a bag."

Kerri met Joan at the nurse's station and briefly explained the plan. "So, I will be back in a little bit to pick her up. Will you still be here?"

"I don't think so hun. I have to go back to Summer's and get my things and then I'll be hitting the road. You guys will be just fine."

The first thing Kerri did when she got to her place was jump in the shower to try to remove the smell of hospital from her skin. She lingered, allowing the hot water to wash away the tension from her body and the doubts from her mind. The water started to run cold, snapping her back to reality and forcing her out of the shower.

Kerri rushed around her apartment, grabbing a couple of dress shirts, a few pairs of jeans and a pair of pajamas. She wasn't sure how long she would be staying but she could pick up other things as she needed them. She threw the bag into the back seat of her car and was about to drive away when the familiar buzz of a text message vibrated on her thigh.

They're releasing me now. Can you meet us out front?
Kerri quickly replied.
On the way now. Be there in a few.

Kerri pulled her seatbelt over her shoulder as she pulled out of her parking spot and onto the road. As she drove Kerri started mentally compiling a list of the things she would need to do when they got to Summer's house and wondered how hard it would be to get a car seat in the back of her two-door car. "Yet another thing that seems to be the universe telling me that I shouldn't have been trying to look cool." She huffed.

Kerri juggled Ava in her car seat, her bag, and Summer's bag as Summer unlocked the door of the house. Kerri ambled in behind her to see very few things out of order, despite the police searching the place the night before. "Joan must have cleaned up after the search. That ticks one thing off my to-do list." Kerri laid the bag by the door and put Ava's carrier up on the coffee table. She opened the fridge to find it fully stocked and discovered a note on the countertop from Joan.

Kerri,

I tried to make this as easy as possible for you both. I did the shopping yesterday and everything has been put back in place. There is a fresh box of diapers in Summer's room for the baby and I put clean sheets on the bed in the spare room, in case that is where you are staying. If you need anything at all, don't hesitate to call.

Joan

Kerri smiled. She should have known that Joan would take care of the little things before her daughter was sent home. Kerri took Ava out of the carrier as Summer came around the corner, grinning at them once again. "What? Did I do something?"

Summer laughed. "Not at all, you just seem so maternal with her in your arms. I never expected it, that's all."

"Well, neither did I. Shouldn't you be lying down?"

"Not until you at least give me a chance to show you around." Summer grasped her hand around Kerri's bicep and started to lead her on a tour of the house.

It was bigger than it looked from the outside with a living room, bedroom and den on the main level, along with the kitchen and dining room area. On the second floor there were two guest bedrooms and the master with its own bathroom.

Summer led Kerri into the closest guest room. "This can be yours, if you like. It's right across the hall from me and Ava, so you will hear her if she cries or me if I need your help."

"Sounds perfect, now will you please get into some PJs and into bed. I'm not going to have you wind up back in the hospital because you refused to rest."

Summer nodded and rolled her eyes. "Okay, okay. I'll go to bed. You sure you are going to be able to manage her until the babysitter arrives?"

"We'll be just fine, won't we Ava?" Kerri bounced her on her side. "We're going to cook up something for mom to eat and see how deep your love of country music goes."

Things went smoothly throughout the weekend as Kerri cooked meals, did laundry and learned about changing diapers and giving baths from the babysitter and the nanny. She had only needed to get up in the night on one occasion to help Summer, and even though she thought that she would, she didn't mind at all.

The next week went by in a blur, but by the following weekend, Kerri had the routines down to a science and Summer was able to do more to help out. When Kerri arrived home from work on Friday evening, Summer had even surprised her by sending Ava with the babysitter for the night and had a homecooked meal on the table.

They were starting to act like a real family. Kerri and Summer had not talked about their relationship over the two weeks that Kerri was playing caretaker and despite some looks exchanged between the two that said they were both thinking about it, neither brought it up. Kerri was still trying not to put pressure on Summer, instead

she hoped they would naturally get back to a more romantic place once Summer was fully healed.

"Well, that was really nice. I don't think I have ever
come home to dinner on the table." Kerri laughed.

"I'm sorry that I'm not a very good cook." Summer
shook her head at the mound of leftover food in the middle of the table.

"Don't be silly. You just overdid it on the amount for
the two of us, I think." Kerri winked.

"I was hoping you might like to sit and watch a movie
with me, like old times?"

"You really must be feeling better. I haven't seen you
watch more than a few minutes of the news without getting a headache."

"My head hasn't bothered me all day. Besides, we
should enjoy the fact that the Ava is out of the house for
the night. I usually only get one night like this a month."

"If you insist. Just give me a minute to change into
something a little more comfortable." Kerri ran up the
stairs while Summer set up the DVD.

When Kerri came back downstairs, Summer had laid
out a spread of Cool Ranch Doritos and chocolate covered
raisins along with a bottle of wine. "This feels oddly familiar." Kerri hesitated at the bottom of the steps.

"All of our favourites, or, at least, they used to be, mi-
nus the wine. I think I've picked out the perfect movie
too." Summer smiled coyly at a confused Kerri and turned
on the DVD player to the main screen of The Matrix.

"Well, that's a blast from the past. Didn't we watch
this together when it came out?"

"We sure did. We watched it on our first unofficial
date." Summer patted the sofa for Kerri to sit beside her.
"There is only one difference this time." Summer slipped

her fingers to the back of Kerri's neck and pulled their foreheads together. "This time, I'm not going to let you chicken out. I'm going to make sure that you kiss me." Summer softly pressed her lips to Kerri's.

Kerri deepened the kiss, feeling Summer push back hungrily before breaking their lips apart to catch her breath. "Wow. That was unexpected."

"Now that is out of the way, let's see what Neo is up to." Summer winked and smiled, settling in beside Kerri on the couch.

They were less than an hour in when Kerri realized that Summer was asleep. She turned off the movie and scooped Summer into her arms, carried her up over the stairs and gently laid her in her bed. Kerri pulled the blankets to cover Summer and clicked off the bedside lamp when Summer opened her eyes.

"I'm sorry I fell asleep. I was really enjoying our night together. Will you please stay here with me?" Summer's mumbled; her eyes pleaded up at Kerri.

"I don't think that is a very good idea. You should sleep."

"No, I just want you to lie beside me and hold me. No funny business, I promise. Just the feeling of your skin and sleep." Summer shifted over in the bed and ran her hand over the open place in the bed.

"No funny business!" Kerri wagged her finger, giving in, taking off her jeans and crawling into the bed.

Summer moved toward her, pressing their knees and foreheads together before cupping Kerri's chin in her hands and kissing her softly. She pressed her face into Kerri's chest and closed her eyes. "Just sleep."

CHAPTER 22

It was a month after she was released from hospital that Summer's doctor finally gave the go ahead for her to go back to work. Kerri had fallen into a routine of meal prep, diaper changes and quiet evenings watching television on the couch. Kerri slept in the spare room every night after their movie night. Holding Summer while she slept made Kerri realize that it was too complicated to be so close, wanting her and not being able to be with her. There had been a couple of times that Summer tried to talk to Kerri about it, but she brushed it off in the fear they had allowed their relationship to fall too far into the friend zone.

On Monday morning Kerri volunteered to drop Ava at the babysitters before heading to work so Summer could have few extra minutes to get ready for her first day. In truth, she wanted to speak to the sitter about the chance that Ava could have an overnight that wasn't on the schedule. Kerri didn't want any interruptions that evening as Summer told her about her first day and Kerri talked about moving back to her own place and what that would mean for them.

That evening, Kerri left work early to put together a three-course meal for what she believed would be her last night staying at Summer's. The second she walked in the door Kerri started work to get her prime rib roast in the oven as she knew it was Summer's favourite. She put their appetizer salad on the table and was fussing with the bottle of wine the lady at the liquor store suggested as a pairing. Kerri wasn't a big fan of wine, but she knew that the red had to breathe, and she wanted the evening to be perfect. Kerri placed the bottle and a pair of glasses on the kitchen island just as Summer breezed in through the front door.

Summer tossed her jacket on the back of the couch as she strolled across the living room. "Honey, I'm home," she laughed.

"In the kitchen." Kerri replied, shaking her head.

"Something smells good. I hope you didn't go to too much trouble." Summer smiled.

Kerri looked around at the mess of dishes in the sink and shrugged. She poured a glass of wine and handed it to Summer. "No trouble at all. I just wanted you to have a nice relaxing evening after your first day back in the real world."

"Well, it looks like you have been hard at work in here. Is Ava napping?"

"Actually, she is out with the babysitter for the night. We have the house all to ourselves because we have a couple of things to celebrate. First of all, cheers to your first day back!" Kerri finished pouring herself a glass of the wine and clinked her glass to Summer's.

"Why, thank you. It was a lot less tiring than I had expected. And what else are we celebrating?"

"Well," Kerri looked at her feet and blushed, "remember when I told you that Steph submitted me and Julia for that national award?"

Summer started to grin, "yeah... I remember..."

"Well, we found out this afternoon that we won!"

Summer placed her glass on the island and grabbed Kerri by the hands. "That's amazing! I mean, I had no doubt that you would win it, but I'm so proud of you! I'm surprised you didn't invite Julia over to celebrate with us!"

"No, I ah, I have something else that I want to talk you about tonight. Besides, she has been here working with me almost every night this week. You didn't need her in your face again, and to be honest, neither did I."

"Something you want to talk about? That sounds ominous. What's up?" Summer unbuttoned the jacket of her business suit and the top button on her blouse, seating herself at the kitchen island.

"After dinner, the first course is being served. First, I want to hear all about your day."

Summer rambled excitedly all through the meal about the cases she was assigned and how encouraging everyone at the office was about her recovery. It was the first time in a while that she did not mention Doug or the upcoming trial. Summer became quiet as Kerri cleared the dessert plates from the table and shared the last of the bottle of wine between them.

"So, I guess now is when we have to talk." Summer swirled the wine in her glass.

"It's nothing bad, really. I just want to tell you that I think it is time that I move back home. I've been here almost four weeks and I'm sure you are ready to have your space back. Besides, Ava is getting attached and I don't know if that is a good idea." Kerri brushed her bang out of her eyes.

"Oh. Yeah, I suppose I hadn't thought about the fact

that you staying here to help had an expiry date. I do really like having you here and you are so great with Ava."

"I like being here. But I'd also like to give us a real chance. Right now, you seem to look at me more as a nanny and a nurse maid. Other than the one night that you kissed me and fell asleep on the couch, you haven't, I mean, I didn't either, but..."

"That's what this is about? I invited you in. You spent the night in my room and then didn't mention it again and never so much as came through the door again unless it was to pick up Ava. I thought I did something wrong, or that you didn't feel comfortable or something. I know that nothing was going to happen that night, but I thought I made it clear that it wasn't because I didn't want you." Summer slammed her wine glass on the table.

"You were hurt. I didn't want to put pressure on you to figure us out until you were recovered and ready. You didn't do anything wrong." Kerri stood from the table and paced the floor. "I'm sorry I made you feel that way."

"I have been feeling fine for more than a week now. You could have said something?"

"I didn't want to be one of those people that has to process everything to death. I figured if something happened naturally that was great, but if not, once I was out of your house, I would ask you out and we could figure things out." Kerri rubbed the back of her neck and stared at the floor.

Summer got up from the table and moved toward Kerri, "How's this for happening naturally?" She placed her hands on either side of Kerri's face and pulled her into a kiss.

Kerri returned the kiss hungrily, grabbing Summer by the collar of her shirt and pulling her into the living room and onto the couch. Summer stopped suddenly, breaking free from the kiss. "No more talking. I have a better idea." She flipped off her shoes, unbuttoned her blouse and let it slip to the floor as she walked to the stairs and motioned for Kerri to follow.

Kerri hesitated before following a trail of clothing that led into Summer's room. Her heart was beating faster with every step and her hands were shaking by her sides, anticipating what she would find when she reached the doorway. She paused in the frame and watched as Summer pulled the straps of her bra over her shoulders and let it fall to the floor before unzipping her skirt and letting it land with it.

Kerri's every action was fueled by the longing. The longing to lose herself in Summer, to feel the touch of Summer's hands on her body, the longing for the weight of Summer's body on hers, the heat of their flesh pressed together and for the softness of Summer's skin beneath her fingertips. She had barely managed to close the door of the room when she grabbed Summer around the waist from behind and gently pressed her lips to the back of her neck and along her exposed shoulder.

Summer sighed loudly, reaching behind her and running her hand through Kerri's hair and along her neck. She dropped her shoulder, bringing her lips to Kerri's and turned to face her. Summer ran her hands along Kerri's sides and under the edge of her shirt, pulling it up her back and stepping back slightly to pull the shirt over Kerri's head before running her hands around her body and quickly unsnapping her bra at the back.

Kerri's arms dropped back to her sides and Summer took her by the hands, holding constant eye contact and pressing her back to the door before kissing her again, harder this time. Kerri jumped with surprise as Summer pinned her arm to the wall above her head and pressed her lips to the side of Kerri's neck.

Kerri whimpered in gratitude as Summer's lips wandered down her chest, sucking gently at her nipple. Summer reached between their bodies, undoing the button on Kerri's baggy jeans and moaning a little as they immediately hit the floor. She ran her fingertips along the edge of Kerri's underwear, slipping her hands inside and grabbing the cool flesh of her ass.

Kerri threw her head back with pleasure as their bodies collided and Summer's nipples rubbed against her chest. She could feel the heat from between Summer's thighs increase as their bodies rubbed together and Kerri shifted her hands to Summer's lower back, trying to take control.

"I don't think so, miss." Summer giggled, thrusting her hips forward just enough to put Kerri off balance before grabbing her by the front of the underwear and pulling her toward the bed. Summer placed her finger under Kerri's chin, tilting her head up to kiss her again quickly before pushing her down onto the bed.

"Well, this is a side of you I've never seen before." Kerri pulled herself up onto her elbows as Summer straddled herself over her.

"Do you like it?" Summer teased. "I can be aggressive too, you know." She winked and threw Kerri's arms above her head before kissing her again.

Kerri rolled her hips, throwing Summer down next to her on the bed, finally managing to take control. Summer pouted through a smile, "But I was having so much fun."

Kerri looked her in the eyes, "But I can't wait any longer to taste you."

Summer gasped as Kerri's lips floated across her neck, down her chest and slowed as she pressed them along her stomach and hip bones. Summer's body shuddered with anticipation, and the words felt shaky as they left her mouth, "I've never let anyone do this."

Kerri ran her hand up Summer's stomach, and grabbed on to her hand. "Do you want me to stop?" She continued to press her lips to the soft skin of her thigh.

"No, I just want you to stop playing and do it." Summer ran her hand through Kerri's hair as Kerri looked up at her in surprise before placing her lips softly against Summer's folds.

Summer inhaled sharply as Kerri continued to kiss lower before gently running her tongue along her clit, pulling it into her mouth and softly sucking while using her tongue to lap up Summer's wetness.

Summer moaned and her hips rolled forward, increasing the pressure. Kerri hummed softly sending vibrations and further arousing Summer. "Oh god, Ker. Please, please make it happen. It's so intense."

Kerri increased the speed of her tongue and gripped onto Summer's hips as she could no longer hold her body still. Within seconds Kerri felt a river wash over her chin and Summer moaned and whimpered in ecstasy. Kerri licked up the mess she had made gently, feeling Summer's body shudder with each flick of her tongue.

"Sorry, you taste so good that I couldn't let it go to waste." She smiled shyly and crawled up the bed, letting her body fall, half against the heat of Summer's body and half against the coolness of the sheets. Kerri brushed her fingers across Summer's lips and jaw. "You okay?"

"So much better than that." Summer sighed and pulled Kerri's face to hers, kissing her tenderly then licked her lips to taste what Kerri had. She groaned and kissed her harder, stroking the back of her fingers over Kerri's side. "My turn." She bit her lip and looked into Kerri's eyes for approval.

"You don't have to." Goosebumps formed on Kerri's shoulders. "It's okay."

Summer kissed just above her bellybutton and smiled up at her. "Oh, but I want to." Summer continued down Kerri's body, trailing her tongue across her skin.

Kerri felt the warmth of Summer's tongue against her, "I'm so close already." She closed her eyes and focusing on the softness of Summer's tongue as it navigated to her most sensitive places. One quick flick and Kerri moaned with pleasure, thrusting her hips forward as she felt a release within her.

Summer wiped her chin and moved up the bed to lie beside Kerri. A single tear rolled down Kerri's cheek and Summer gently wiped it away, breathing hard into Kerri's neck, letting her lips brush against the sweat on Kerri's skin. Kerri turned to look at her and Summer placed her hand on the side of her face so their lips could meet once again.

Kerri was never more present than when their lips met in that moment. She felt an intensity and a love that she had never experienced before. They lay together, spent from the passion and the exertion, limbs entwined. Kerri listened as Summer struggled to calm her breathing and could feel the beat of her own heart still pounding in her chest. She couldn't move in that moment, even if she wanted to.

Summer gently stroked her fingers over Kerri's exposed stomach, "This probably isn't the right time, but can I ask you something?"

Kerri sighed and pressed her lips to the top of Summer's head. "Nothing hard, okay? My brain isn't working quite right after that."

Summer chuckled, "Move in with me. For real."

Kerri reached down and tilted up Summer's chin, "I thought you would never ask."

Summer rolled over and glanced at the clock on her nightstand over Kerri's shoulder. "I know you hate it, but happy birthday."

Kerri blushed. "This might have jumped the line as my best birthday ever."

Summer brushed her lips against Kerri's exposed shoulder. "I'm glad. Sleep now?"

"Mmm hmmm. Definitely."

CHAPTER 23

The final day of Doug's trial arrived after months of testimony and the presentation of the evidence that police had collected to connect him to The Closet Murders. Summer was to be the last person to testify for the prosecution. Kerri dropped Ava with the babysitter early and headed home to get ready to go to court. She had taken the day off work to support Summer, so Julia would have to cover this part of the trial alone.

Kerri's palms were sweating, but Summer seemed perfectly calm as they climbed the steps of the courthouse. "I know you go to court all the time, but I thought you would be more nervous having to testify."

Summer just smiled. "I'm just glad that once I get through this, it will all be over. No more prepping for what I am going to say, no more going over and over the incident in my mind. I won't ever have to relive it on purpose after this."

"I suppose. I just don't know how I would feel if I had to sit up there, face him, and talk about what he did. I definitely wouldn't be as cool as you seem." Kerri squeezed Summer's hand.

"I'm not as cool as you think. I just hide it well. This is going to be one of the hardest things I have ever done, but it will be okay because you are going to be right there with me." Summer squeezed back.

Julia was the first person they saw when they walked into the court room. They had become good friends since Kerri officially moved in with Summer. Kerri and Julia had been working closely together throughout the trial and would often set up camp in the living room to prep for the next day so that Kerri didn't have to spend late nights at the office. Summer would also bring her work home and set up in the dining room, so Ava spent less time with a babysitter.

Julia was seated near the back of the court with a recorder in one hand and her note pad set out beside her on the bench. "Well, if it isn't North Beach's great power couple." Julia smiled and stood to hug the pair.

Summer laughed. "That's us. How are things going with that new girl of yours? Kerri tells me you actually went on not only a second, but a third date with this one?"

"Yep. Looks like I might be settling down in my old age. I just took your advice and gave it a real chance. It sure does make things a little strange around the office though."

Summer raised an eyebrow at the comment. "Why is that?"

Kerri laughed, "I guess I forgot to mention that part. This new girl in her life is our boss."

"Steph?" Summer's jaw dropped in shock.

"Guilty! I have been flirting with that woman since my first day on the job, I didn't realize she was flirting back until Kerri pointed it out. But it's going well, so far. Kerri is the only one at work that knows, but it is hard not to act differently around her."

"You guys are so obvious," Kerri poked Julia in the ribs. "You're goony over each other, it's gross!"

Julia pointed between Kerri and Summer, "Look who's talking!"

"I'm surprised the whole world hasn't figured it out." Kerri teased again.

"Well, she makes me happy. I think we could really have something."

"Then we should have you both over for dinner. As soon as this is all over, that is." Summer gestured around the courtroom.

They quickly took their seats as the prosecution entered the room, followed by the defense team. Doug was led in by a police officer, clad in orange and handcuffs that bound his feet and hands. Summer shuddered and Kerri rubbed her back in reassurance. No matter how prepared Summer may be and how much she was looking forward to it being over, Kerri wasn't sure she was ready to hear Summer talk about it again.

The courtroom fell into a hush as the judge was announced. A low voice boomed through the room, "The prosecution calls Summer Donnelly-Peters to the stand." Kerri shifted uncomfortably in her seat as Summer stood and made her way to the front.

Kerri could only hear the pounding of her heart in her ears as Summer pledged to tell the truth and her mind drifted back to the night that she had found out that Summer was in the hospital fighting for her life. She never could have imagined in that moment that this would be where they would find themselves eight months later.

Kerri's mind continued to wander back over the last several months, her and Summer raising Ava together, all the little moments they had shared. She thought about the

night she called Jack to tell him they were moving in together.

"*I figured it was only a matter of time. I get to be best man
at the wedding, right?*" Jack teased.

"*We're nowhere near talking about that, bro. Just tell me
that I'm doing the right thing and that you are happy for me?*"
Kerri pleaded.

"*Of course, I'm happy for you, but only you know if it is
the right thing. It's the thing you have wanted since you were
young, to settle down with someone. I even watched you try it
once before, but the fact that you never got over Summer always
stopped you from being truly happy. This is your chance to see if
you can and if you think it is the right move, I'm all for it.*"

"*You always know how to say exactly what I need to
hear.*"

"*I'm your brother, I know you best. I have to run, talk
soon?*"

"*Sure. Love you Jack.*"

Kerri tore herself from the memory in time to hear the
prosecutor excuse the witness. Summer looked pale as
she made her way back to her seat, gathered her coat and
left the room. Kerri quickly stood to follow her, nodding
at Julia as they passed and gesturing for her to call them
with an update on the case.

Kerri followed silently behind Summer as they made
their way across the parking lot and Kerri jumped in the
driver's side of the car. She placed the key in the ignition
but didn't turn it as Summer adjusted herself and put on
her seatbelt.

"Do you want to talk about it?" Kerri choked out, staring forward through the windshield.

"There is nothing left to say. Even though I know it
isn't true, it feels like this nightmare is over for me. I got

to look him in the face and tell him what he did to me and what pain his actions will cause his daughter in the future."

"You're going to explain this to Ava?" Kerri puzzled.

"Someday. She is going to have questions about her father, and I have been thinking about it a lot, I don't want us to lie to her about it."

Kerri nodded. "I will tell her as much or as little as you want when the time comes. I think we have a few years before we need to start worrying about that, though, so this isn't a conversation we need to be having."

"Not right now, anyway. I'm kinda tired and I have a headache. Do you mind if we just go home so I can lie down? The prosecution will rest this afternoon and the jury will be sent to deliberate. You never know how long that is going to take so it could be days before we hear anything." Summer rubbed her temples and around to the back of her head.

Kerri held Summer until she went to sleep, listening to her breath. When she was sure that Summer was out, Kerri finally let the sobs that had been hanging in the back of her throat burst from her mouth. Tears of sadness for the families of the victims she had seen in the courtroom and for Summer who had survived flooded her cheeks. She held Summer a little tighter, wiping her face in the back of her t-shirt and closed her eyes.

Kerri was woken by the sound of her phone buzzing on the nightstand. She gently slipped her arm out from in under the pillow that Summer was sleeping on, careful not to disturb her. It was a text from Julia.

The jury is back. They are calling everyone in for the verdict.

"Sum, honey. Time to get up, we have to get back to

court."

Summer groaned and rolled over, looking at the clock. "Already?"

"Yeah. Julia messaged. I thought it was fast. Is that a good thing?"

Summer nodded sleepily, "Usually."

The courtroom was packed when they entered. They managed to squeeze into a row with a family Kerri recognized as belonging to the first victim and one of the police officers that had been a primary on the investigation. Kerri held her breath as the jury was seated and the court was called to order.

"Ladies and gentlemen of the jury, have you reached a verdict?" The judge reached out to take a piece of paper handed to him by the bailiff and nodded as he read it. "Would the defendant please stand?"

Kerri looked over at Summer who was sitting with her eyes closed, hands clasped together in her lap. She reached out and placed her hand on Summer's knee, squeezing to remind her that she was still beside her. After what felt like an eternity, the judge began to read the decision.

"Douglas Andrew Peters, on four counts of first-degree murder, the jury finds you guilty." Sighs of relief could be heard throughout the court. The judge continued, "On the charge of aggravated assault, the jury finds you guilty and on the charge of attempted murder, the jury finds you guilty as charged." The judge banged his gavel.

Summer buried her face in her hands and her chest heaved with sobs. Kerri pulled her into her chest and rocked her like a baby as the tears continued to flow. Kerri kissed the top of her head and stroked her hair, knowing she needed this release as Kerri had needed it before.

"It's okay, baby. I got you." Kerri kissed the top of her

head again and continued to rock Summer as the other observers moved from the benches and hugged each other before filtering out into the hall.

They were left alone on their bench until Julia sat beside Summer, placing her hand on Summer's shoulder and nodding at Kerri. "He is going away for a long, long time. You did that. Your words were so compelling that they had to convict. You should be so proud of yourself; we are so proud of you."

Summer's breathing started to slow as she composed herself. Julia handed Summer a tissue, clutched Kerri's hand and smiled before getting up, "I should get to work. This story won't write itself. But I'll see you ladies soon?"

Kerri nodded, "Absolutely, maybe dinner on the weekend, if that isn't too soon?"

"Sounds good. Take care Summer," Julia picked up her belongings, leaving them as the only people remaining in the courtroom.

Summer looked up at Kerri. "I'm sorry about that. I'm okay, really." Summer took Kerri by the hand as she stood and led her out of the room.

They lingered and observed people in the hall for a few minutes, watching victim's families congratulate each other and discuss their impact statements for the sentencing. Summer hadn't tried to bond with them. She had told Kerri she didn't want to get too close in case it was uncomfortable or awkward for them. Although she was a victim, she was also the wife of the man that had killed their daughters and she had no idea what he was doing. She smiled and shook hands with a few people before Kerri dragged her out into the street.

"How do you feel? Now that it is all over?"

"Like we can really go on with our lives. Like we can

finally put this all behind us and be truly happy." Summer put her arms around Kerri's waist and pulled her close, kissing her forehead. "I can't wait to really start my life with you."

Kerri rubbed her hands down over Summer's arms, kissing her quickly as she brought her hands from around her waist and held them. Kerri reached into her pocket and pulled out a small box before taking a knee. "Marry me?"

"I thought you would never ask."

ABOUT THE AUTHOR

Sarah Thompson is a former radio broadcaster and journalist from Grand Falls-Windsor, NL.

She was first published in the Engen Books compilation *light|dark* in 2010 with the science fiction story 'Remers.'

Sarah currently owns and operates her own dinner theatre business for which she writes the shows, including *Leroy's Diner*, *Going to the Chapel*, and, *I'll Be Home For Christmas*.

She is a big fan of the community theatre scene and can often be found performing or directing with the Off Broadway Players. Sarah lives with her wife and dog, Roger, in Corner Brook, Newfoundland.

The Love of Summer is her first novel.

www.ingramcontent.com/pod-product-compliance
Lightning Source LLC
Chambersburg PA
CBHW011427010726
47494CB00011B/2545